Diary of a
Witch Doctor

by
T.J. Westcott

Diary of a Witch Doctor

Copyright © 2014, T.J. Westcott

Line Edit by Chris Smith

Cover Art by ProBookCovers.com

ACKNOWLEDGEMENTS

Special thanks to friends and family for your encouragement, Skip Press for your invaluable insight and suggestions, Chris Smith for the timely line edit, Travis Miles at ProBookCovers.com for your diligence in the cover design creation, T.J. Garrison for the thoughts, and to all Emergency Department doctors and nurses everywhere who are charged with keeping hope alive where it is often in short supply. Most especially to Lori and Monica for your patience and understanding.

ENTRY 1

Let me first say that I'm not crazy but you'd beg to differ if you peered into my cell. A small hospital bed with only a stripped down bare plastic mattress – the teeth mark punctures upon it aren't mine, I swear. The plain steel bedframe's only accents were those of the iron loops welded to it to anchor the four-point leather restraints. No furniture. The blades of the ceiling fan that never stop turning caused an incessant whir, as if trying to wick away not only the beads of perspiration from my throbbing forehead but the frustrations and anxieties that have clouded my mind these dozen years. This is where I, myself, have put the nut burgers, whack-jobs, cretins and the other assorted wounded of society. Maybe even *you*? You probably are wounded too. Nobody's unscathed, except maybe Jeff Logan.

He was my best friend long before he got me sprung from my little 'lapse in judgment,' an event that caused me to take up this journal. I figured that writing a few coherent sentences would help backup the claim that the brain cells still call and talk, even if you're tired of listening to the conversation.

Kind of like trying to discern what to listen to in the noisy E.R. with its cantankerous moaners, crying babies, and cursing drunks that take turns singing lead to the orchestral cacophony of chaos. Supported by a rhythm section of beeps and chirps of equipment alarms and check switches, I am its maestro. Walk-running between rooms conducting the team, handing off one chart into an approaching nurse's hands as I simultaneously grasp another from a nurse traveling in the opposite direction. I cover everything as I think, just this one more patient and maybe I'll be able to take a leak before 9:00 a.m.!

This morning, however, was to be no different as another's organ decided to mangle the tempo.

"Name?" I ask.

"Not registered yet," said Nurse Sierra, "She was a little wheezy at the hair salon yesterday per family."

The craggy faced old lady's lungs wheezed like demented bagpipes. As the nurses started the IV's, I waved in the respiratory therapists who went to work administering oxygen through a BVM (bag, valve, mask) apparatus.

"My -- name -- I can't, I -- just..." were her only utterances, and all ignored. To engage her would have only tired her further and I had already cracked the airway box jump kit from its wall support. I gave the laryngoscope a little wrist flick, its long metallic blade locked into position, igniting its tiny fiber optic light tip, as I called for the Rapid Sequence Induction kit that contained the meds needed to sedate and paralyze the patient for me to give her the *plastic cigar.*

"We'll just call you our pretty lady," I said, dispensing with names, remembering she had just been to the salon.

But *she* won't remember. Not any of this. The medication will blunt any recollection of the minutes that occurred just before. We've created what evolution has failed to - a way to forget, a 'bridge out' sign that our world-weary minds must obey. If *I* had something like that, I could have avoided the embarrassment of what occurred next.

Nurse Thelma came in from making another contact with the family and provided more information on the patient as I slid the long cold steel blade of the laryngoscope down Pretty Lady's throat. Thelma rattled off the patient's allergies and then unintentionally invoked Murphy's Law. Murphy, was the original emergency medicine physician it's been said.

"…Medical history," she droned, "includes a previous neck injury with a nerve impingement syndrome and multi-level fusion."

I could feel my grip tighten on the laryngoscope's handle as Thelma whispered to Sierra, "I've never seen him shake before." Even more so, I hated the feel of Sierra's gaze studying my now trembling hand. It trembled all the more, now knowing that my inability to manipulate the patient's neck into proper position was hampered by her warped anatomy - making it harder to place the plastic breathing tube into her throat - but more so, at *remembering* - that no good deed went uncrucified.

"It's the malpractice case," Sierra flatly told Thelma.

Damn, that's why I didn't like her. She was the kind of woman who knows things that you'd rather she didn't. Comes in handy for sniffing out the *playahs* who come into the ER but sucked when it smelled *you*.

I still can't see the vocal cords.

"Come on honey, cough up those cords for me," I said out loud, half to relax myself and half to give the staff the impression I was confident even when my mind's eye saw itself sucking my thumb while wetting my pants. I strained and lifted harder on the scope handle trying not to chip a tooth - another lawsuit event, even if I saved her life - and *there,* there were the pearly white vocal cords. The plastic curved airway tube slid right between them with an immediate sense of relief, accomplishment and satisfaction. It was pulmonary orgasm.

Instead of a cigarette, I reached for her clipboard and scribbled out an order for blood gases 'now' and in thirty minutes after the ventilator was hooked up to the breathing tube that was just inserted, while the portable x-ray machine was swung into the room to shoot the obligatory chest film. We all momentarily stepped out of the room as usual for the shoot to avoid having our privates nuked.

Not that it would matter for me, I have no use for mine.

"Are you the doctor? How's my mother?" asked the longhaired twenty-something brunette who was the daughter of Pretty Lady. She munched on a bag of chips nervously as the crumbs disappeared into her cleavage while her other family members tried to work their way around the hospital security guard like defensive linebackers intent on muscling a tired quarterback. Next thing I knew, her Uncle Benny, with yellow teeth and enough ethanol on his breath to gas up a Chevy Suburban, was in my face (*cough, cough*). Sadly, the remainder of the hygienically challenged clan has yet to have discovered the invention of soap. Worse, they had me hemmed in against the wall - my own little perverted paparazzi.

"She'll be on the vent for a few days," I explained trying to slide along the wall away from the breath odor of the liquored up uncle. Stale alcohol breath with stagnant cigarette breath and rotted teeth made the worst foot odor downright pleasant.

My eyes watered at the stench while her daughter's eyes suddenly grew big, "It's not that *Goliath infection* the news has been warning us about?!" she squealed.

"There's not been one case in this country, but the hysteria from the news reports is epidemic," I explained somewhat wearily. You see, long after the news anchors step away from their studio desks, we are left to clarify and debunk all of the "*Urgent Health Alerts,*" the latest drug warnings, "...that may just PRESERVE your LIFE," and health miracles promising a cure for cancer that you then never hear about again.

Sound cynical? I'm a realist. If it's not in a respected peer reviewed medical journal, it ain't happening for me.

Just down the hallway, a man in a dirty T-shirt and leathers stared intensely at me from one of the treatment rooms and shouted, "Hey, doc, what is this? I want a word with you." But I already knew what he wanted. This patient was what we in the pit referred to as a *frequent flyer*. What *I* wanted to know was when did humanity come to accept the belief that by fixing a piercing gaze on the head of a hospital caregiver, he or she would instantly zombify and fulfill your immediate bidding - or at the very least, spontaneously combust like a lit fart.

He wasn't the only one who wanted more than just a word, as Belinda, the E.R. coding biller grabbed my arm, "I really enjoyed last night," she cooed. "Can we do it again sometime?" Her dreamy eyes searched mine, and I knew that look. The "s" word look, and I don't mean sex. S as in *same* person to always go eat with, the *same* person to sleep with, the *same* person that says she loves you and tries to change you when you don't match up to who or what she thought you were. Though usually, I'd have just meant *sex*.

I stalled, "Um, yeah sure. I'll call you sometime. I gotta go." It bothered me that her voice trailed off as she echoed mine with a disappointed, "Sometime?" I was almost thankful that I had to go to face the frequent flyer's wrath.

"Must be -- the fourth date?" Nurse Sierra asked Belinda.

"How did you know?" she replied rather surprised.

"Beats me, never dated him."

And she never would. The Sierras of the world are those who look for the 'something solid.' 'Guarantees' on a planet where the only one is that there are none. It's the prom queen looking for the prom king, but never quite finding him. They don't exist, and the only Princess I've ever found was a stray bitch that had obviously been abused - at least it said so on her collar's license tag: PRINCESS. The little mutt should've been put down, but I hid her in my apartment for weeks and fattened her up on leftover lunches missed while on duty. Rather than track her owner, I left her in a kid's wagon - one who I once treated after a careless speedster driver hit her and her dog. (She made it, her dog didn't.) "What is *this*?!" I remembered her mother exclaiming at the furry discovery that sat there giving her the blinking puppy eyes from the wagon.

"What the fuck *is* this?" the man in the dirty T-shirt and leathers growled, snapping me back to the present moment as he rudely waved in my face with his good hand the prescription I wrote for him. His sprained other wrist was still in a splint.

"You haven't met my needs," he went on, "you showed no concern at all."

"I agree."

"The most uncaring… wait, what?"

"You're right. I won't feed your habit. I'm not your dealer. I gave you ibuprofen instead for your wrist injury," I said, while I reached around to grab his old charts from the rack outside the treatment room door, half to offer proof of my claim, half to make certain I was close enough to the doorway for a viable escape should he suddenly jerk-out on me. "Oh, and what have we here? Why it's your old chart! Hmm," I mocked as I read, "…wants Vicodin for toothache. Thirteen times - for a toothache!" I stared back at him before going back to the file. "Says ibuprofen 'doesn't work' and needs something stronger for other - nonexistent - injuries, eight times. Shall I continue?"

I didn't need to. He threw the prescription paper onto the floor. I had busted him. Most of my colleagues would've just let him get up and walk out, like he was doing just at that moment. Not me.

"Do you need help with a drug problem?" I continued as I followed him out the treatment room door. Silence was his only reply. Until, that is, he thought himself a gong percussionist by creating an obnoxious bang on the exit door with his 'injured wrist' that was too tender to touch or even move, just moments before.

Taking note, I threw my head back and outstretched my arms to Heaven. "He's healed! Another miracle! Amen, brothers and sisters! Come back tomorrow when our nursing staff performs *A Chorus Line*, walking on water!" I'm always happy to *out* a drug seeker. They're a pox on the system, taking staff and resources from those who truly need them. Not that they don't need help and repair of whatever problems, real or imagined that they have, but when they're only interested in the charade...no thanks.

I walk-ran toward the next room. We can't delay. We're tracked on every minute from door-to-doctor time, to the time a patient's admitted or released. Take too long and you could get a reprimand or worse. I paused briefly when I saw one of the newer nurses bending over, next to a treatment cart in one of the rooms. She looked for a vein in her patient's arm for an IV start.

"Go lower with the arm," I coached from the hall, "let it hang below the body, it'll make the veins stand out more." As she took my advice, she bent over further and her uniform scrub top billowed out from gravity to reveal the tops of her voluptuous breasts. "*Nice* work Dr. Feldman," I murmured to myself. Yeah, that's the field to have gone into - Plastics. Where patients are happy. Happy to see you and are always sober. I cursed my lack of R&R time.

Mental gears shifted again in the suture room as I lined up my target area to anesthetize a jagged laceration on a child's shoulder. "Just a little prick with a needle," I tried to soothe - this always got a laugh when I'd say it to a big bad-ass biker - and just like that, the needle went in. But in that moment, the little bugger snapped his head around and drew my blood, leaving a nice impression of his overbite in my hand. The nurse in the room looked up fearfully. She's seen first hand the results of my feelings toward the biting or abuse of staff members. I surprised her by just breathing and calmly disinfecting the bite. Her eyes got all the bigger when I reached in my pocket and came up with -

"Stickers!" called the little knuckle biter.

"Those were axed from the budget," the nurse said coyly.

"I know you were just scared," I told the boy, as his disposition morphed from rabid beast back to child, "I know. …Don't do that again. "

ENTRY 2

Where kids at times may act like wild monkeys, it's the suit apes that are the most annoying of the species. They usually descend suddenly, in a troop, noses up as if sniffing the air to detect any target at which to throw their fecal criticisms to justify their wage. Knuckles dragging over clipboard edges making copious notes, their low toned grunts keep employees guessing and working.

One of these creatures seemed to try to save me from myself at times - Jeff Logan. Even though I've studied him - Jane Goodall would've been so proud - I still couldn't figure out if it was because he's a decent fellow or that he got some sadistic pleasure out of seeing his former college buddy toil in blood and vomit, while he admired his secretary's silhouette reflected on the glass protector of his business administration degree in his plush office. At that particular moment, he fidgeted nervously with reports tucked under his arm while he followed behind Mark Henley, the Medical Director and the Vice President, Kels Mitchall.

"Look, I know you're concerned about his Speilman/Cox/Pennis Customer Satisfaction Rating, but I think he's just going through a rough time because he has to get ready for his malpractice case coming up soon," Jeff rattled.

"We know you two go back to college days, but friends or not, customers aren't happy, and this must be addressed," droned Kels.

I tried to avoid eye contact by picking up a patient's chart to pretend to study. Of course, I *would* pick up one that's *blank* - crap. Mark spoke up in that calm firm voice physicians use to try to set themselves as the top banana, "Nate, we'd like a word with you."

"Dum-dum-dum-dummm."

"It's about your customer satisfaction scores," said Jeff, slowing down.

"*Patient* satisfaction scores," I corrected. Customers are always right. Patients need care. At least that's what I've always been taught. Sadly, suit apes have never been able to wrap their prehensile minds around this distinction.

Kels continued, "It's not about your medical expertise, rather --"

"-- You're severely deficient, again, in personalized service sectors," Mark interjected.

"I try to keep people alive. I hold a family member's quivering hand when their loved one dies. How much more personalized can I get?" I asked. I mean have you ever seen one of those old vaudeville clips? The ones where some doofus runs back and forth in front of seven or so tall thin sticks, all in a line, upon which he tries to keep a dinner plate spinning on the tip of each without it falling off and crashing to the floor? That's kinda my job. Running and spinning. Keep 'em all spinning without letting anyone fall and break. Speaking of which, I began to notice things backing up due to the suit apes' little interruption.

"Under this question here," said Jeff, as he pointed to one of the pages he plucked from the stack, "Did the doctor greet you *promptly* with a warm smile?"

"Very low across the board," noted Mark.

Down here in the pit, my time is not my own. It belongs to the sickest and, "Who wants a grinning idiot?" I asked.

"Obviously the customers who filled out this questionnaire," said Kels.

Not to be deterred, I blurted out somewhat softly, "*Patients.*"

"We want to post better scores than our competing hospitals," Mark said.

Now this, to me, is the epitome of stupid. Like it's some kind of race. I always felt lawyers and medical entities should have never been allowed to advertise in the first place. I mean, aren't we all just interested in helping the patient get the best care? I could feel my blood pressure rising, "Look, we keep people alive in all this chaos, work long hours and treat everyone - no matter how sick, drunk, crazy or *hungry* they may be," I said as I held up my bitten, bandaged hand. But I could see I wasn't getting through. Especially to Kels, who only smugly deadpanned, "You need to be more warm and entertaining for each and every customer."

"Entertaining? Entertaining?"

There was no answer to my query. Nor did I expect there to be. The Great Ape had spoken. That was that. What happened next was rather a blur. I began to grind my teeth. I had barely caught my breath from a Sheriff's deputy handing me a subpoena - damn things flow like water in the ER - to testify as medical witness in a child abuse case when I noticed a female patient. Her jaws worked on the beef jerky stick she pulled from her purse while calmly inquiring of the nurse, "Excuse me, but did that patient die?"

At this I spun and witnessed, through the door of the trauma room, my colleague - Dr. Sashire – take off his gloves while a nurse disconnected the monitor wires from the dead patient. "She did," the nurse replied to the jerky jerk, a tinge of regret in her voice.

"Well then, that patient doesn't need any more care, now do they, so the doctor can just come over here and take care of my sinus infection and stuffy nose."

I felt my blood boil. My sanity yet again stained by this witnessed 'low' perpetrated by my species, one charged with the capacity for empathy, above all creatures. All this, while the senile old patient from cart-C shuffled by, completely naked with his rod and the twins swaying as he walked. He held his wadded-up gown in his hand without so much as a raised eyebrow on his face, or that of the staff.

"Your lawyer's on line three," the ward clerk called to me. Suddenly my mind couldn't take the soul bleaching fatigue, the overload. Each and every beep from a cardiac monitor was like a spike driven into my skull. The moans, sobs and shrieks, conjured a mind eye's image of Dante's poetic, *Inferno*. In the middle of that scene, all I saw was Kels' smile. Like a beaming, mocking Chesire Cat and I was its kill.

In a foggy rage, I blocked the exit of a discharged patient carrying prescriptions in one hand and his portable music player in another, "May I, for a moment?" I half-heartedly asked, "Thank you." Before he could answer a word, my thumb had already flipped the switch 'on' and the music pumped loudly, vibrating a patient's water cup off the counter ledge where I had rested the player. Its contents spilled into the desktop computer screen monitor that gagged in a flash and puff of smoke, as it gave up its pixilated ghost. I jumped onto the counter through the smoke, halting the player from launching itself over the vibrating edge and yelled, "You want entertainment? I *give* you entertainment." Dancing wildly, arms flailing, pelvis thrusting and legs going in opposite directions, off came my scrub top.

Jeff shouted my name, trying to get me to stop but to which I danced all the more, waving my ass in his face. I saw Nurse Kiley come to stand next to Nurse Sierra. They watched the spectacle of my gyrating hips swivel the drawstrings of my scrub pants, like pastie tassels on the breasts of a gawky stripper.

"I call 'briefs,' I hope," said Kiley.

"Boxers," added Sierra nonchalantly with an amended assertion of, "definitely."

An ancient lady on a cart nearby craned her neck at the sight of the dancing doctor and smiled a toothless grin at the show. A syringe-packing nurse stood next to her bed and watched this patient's previously slow heart rhythm on the bedside monitor display pick up speed. With a jaded eye roll, she tossed the cardiac medication filled syringe into the dirty sharps container, the need for dysrhythmia medication now abated. I blew kisses -

one to the old lady, then one to everybody. To my left and to my right, kisses for all with my top hat a bedpan, a crutch for my cane.

Whoosh! Off came the pants. It was boxers.

Kiley looked disappointed at paying up the bet when the ten-dollar bill was passed to Sierra who was totally unimpressed with the show and, rather matter-of-fact about it all - a battle hardened ER nurse or BHERN (pronounced 'burn') if ever there was one. Just like Nurse Candice - a killer body with beauty to match - who flashed a mischievous smile and whispered to Kiley as she passed behind them, "I would've told you if you just asked." I would have asked Candy, er, Candice to join me on the counter, but then Security rushed in and closed the show.

The last thing I remember was Sierra going toward the end of the hall to assist Dr. Sashire. I screamed some unintelligible lyrics as they dragged me forward by my armpits while the tops of my shoes swept the floor. They were the same lyrics I'd shout after being up all night and seeing too much pain to stay awake for the ride home. She wisely never looked back to see the spectacle. I felt sorry for Sashire's having to pick up the rest of the ER load with my newfound friends taking me out to play. Sashire's a good man. Learned five weeks ago he has AIDS. Got it from helping stitch a stoned and disruptive HIV positive gang member who jerked and caused him to stick himself. Says he's too worn out being scared to worry. He wonders what happens next. He wonders about his kids and his wife. Battle scars for the pit warrior, collateral damage to be suffered by his innocent family.

Before Sierra reached Sashire, she deposited her ten-dollar win into the *Charities for the Disabled* collection jar without pause. Others would have treated themselves with such a prize instead. Sierra was a disappointment after all - too 'perfect' for a BHERN.

ENTRY 3

The clack of the lock on the steel entry door woke me and announced a visitor to my cell. I wondered if this one would have another syringe of haloperidol to shut me up. In came Jeff. He looked down at the four-point leathers that shackled me. Large, thick straps of cowhide with metal buckles and supports for unruly or dangerous patients - one for each wrist and ankle to secure to the bed frame. I could see that Jeff didn't quite know what to say.

"Four points," I observed, "And I don't drink nor drug."

"Maybe you should," he retorted opening the blinds and thus blinded me as the bright light seared my eyes.

"Morning?" I asked somewhat surprised.

"You've slept for almost two days.

"I've worked fourteen hours each the last four."

Jeff walked to the doorway and motioned for the nurse to come in. She held the restraint keys and shook her head disapprovingly before she unlocked my restraints. I guess it's always easiest to act as judge when you hold the keys to another's captivity.

"They told me they were just until you were calmer," Jeff said, nodding at the restraints. Silently, he watched the nurse leave the room lock the door.

"I'm calm. Probably don't have a job anymore," I said.

"They were going to fire you. I suggested that we try to help you instead." That was Jeff, always willing to help his friend, as long as he perhaps got something out of it too. I rubbed my wrists and ankles that were sore from the restraints - being on this side of the cart's rails sucked. Furthermore, at this point, I didn't care anymore. I've waded through more puke and blood than most of my species. I was tired. And perhaps this journal would've closed here, where it started. Except for that one damn thing... Student Loans! Lots of 'em - a second mortgage worth. Can't pay 'em back being a greeter at Walmart, though wouldn't that be fun to see the reaction? "Hi, welcome to Walmart. Basket? And, how about a prostate check? Please *drop 'em* in the Office Supplies aisle next to the rubber fingers display. I'll meet you there," I'd say with friendly wave with a 'smiley face' inked on my index finger.

Medicine was not unlike the fabled Mafia. Once you're in, you're in for life.

"It'd be good for you to get out of the country for a bit. Vacation?" continued Jeff, half trying to help and half seeing if I'd help him to help me.

"No fun alone," I answered.

"You wouldn't be alone."

Jeff let me sit there on the bed rather confused awaiting more as he went back and checked the door one more time to make certain it was secure. He came back and sat next to me. Like when we would hatch something fun back in our college dorm. A conquest. An adventure. But all he began to talk was shop. "Goliath's been all the rage in the news," he said.

"I believe it, I saw five people this week with bronchitis who were scared they had it instead."

Jeff stood up and began to pace as he lowered his voice and spoke resolutely, "Our university research affiliate's come to learn that there's a little known reclusive tribe pushed deep into the African Congo jungle by rebel and government skirmishes. Rumor has it that particular tribe had the Goliath virus pass trough it without any deaths. Not one."

"Rumor?" I asked, "I deal with facts, and I don't see what this has to do with me."

"Administration wants to hastily send a team to check it out. There's nothing even remote to western medicine out there. They'd like a doctor to go, for the team's safety, as well as good will toward the people of the area."

I coolly inquired, "Who volunteered?" so as to gently suggest I wasn't offering, if he was asking.

"Nobody. We had one, but he walked when he heard there were guerrillas in the area."

"Doesn't like apes, huh?" I laughed.

"Not the kind that carry assault rifles. So?" he added.

I knew he likely meant rebels and not 'gorillas' however, my little private joke at mixing up the two just popped faster than a genital abscess on a drunken lap dancer - Jeff was talking serious crap. However, I had enough crap of my own, and put my pants back on and headed for the door and said, "Nah, Detroit Memorial finds enough bullet wounds for me without looking for any of my own." But Jeff only hurried around me to casually block my exit at the door.

"Finding a cure is important to the hospital's prestige, Nate. And the *only* way administration will pull the strings to give you another chance," he said.

Another chance to keep my job, to *avoid* a black mark on my professional record, for a report of treatment for 'mental breakdown' would cost me my practice license. To *avoid* defaulting on all my med school loans that I'm still paying off, another chance to *eat*. Mr. Goodwrench can't be Mr. Goodwrench without a garage. An ER doc needs an ER. It's not like you can set up your own trauma bay in a store front office.

"Seeing as how you have me by the family jewels..." I said, as I looked at my crotch. Yes, my physical manhood was still there though Jeff's jungle excursion demand shrunk them a bit. "Don't damage them," I added with a wince, "only ones I got."

"I'm helping you, Nate," he replied tepidly. Clearly, he knew he had me by the balls.

SUPPLEMENTAL ENTRY

The chartered jet sat quietly on the tarmac away from the rest of the frenetic airport activity. The sun was burning off the early morning fog that added an air of uncertainty as if veiling what lay ahead. Jeff shook off the morning chill as he watched the hard shell equipment cases and trunks - the kind rock stars travel with - get shoved into the belly of the plane. Testing equipment, suitcases, electronics, and satellite phone, medical and emergency supplies, all to aid in the search of a primitive band of natives who largely avoid contact with the outside world. It was believed that if the Goliath virus did pass through the clan without doing damage, it was because of one of two possibilities: Either they had some kind of natural immunity to it or they had found a preventative agent.

Perhaps you'll recall the Goliath virus first appeared about a year ago. Its method of action is rather insidious. The respiratory system is attacked first. Sucked down from airborne particles coughed or sneezed into the air, it then goes to work restricting airways by the excessive phlegm produced as it infects and replicates in the cells of the tracheobronchial tree. Breaking the cells down, they move next to those that line the blood vessels where they kill those cells to obtain a needed protein from them. The problem is, these lining cells of the vascular endothelium also make up factors that play a role in the body and its ability to clot blood. The second, later part of the infection is massive bleeding where if you haven't died from respiratory distress, you will from hemorrhaging spontaneously. Drowning in your own blood.

I watched as Jeff's wife Meg, handed him his small carry-on duffle bag as Mark Henley and Kels Mitchall met them upon the tarmac. Standing with them was a Dr. Turfle, a rather gaunt man whose joints resembled those of a stalk of old bamboo. A medical botanist from the university, he looked like he had become one of his own exotic specimens Mark introduced him to Jeff and Meg.

"Turfle, from Prism Pharmaceuticals?" asked Jeff taking note, "Where's Nate?"

"Formerly," Turfle said, "Until they were brought out and taken over by Preminger."

Kels spotted a rather thin but sinewy dark skinned, college age guy who looked as if he needed a good meal. He sang a soft melody with words I couldn't quite make out, as he helped schlep some of the gear on board. "There's our interpreter-guide," said Kels.

"Here? This side of the ocean?" quizzed Mark, who had thought it better to go ahead and contract with a local guide once there.

"Exchange student. From the university," Jeff clarified.

"Dengon, has our last group member arrived?" Kels asked. Dengon looked up from his schlepping duties and answered, "He's on the plane."

"Idiot. He never showed for the briefing," said Kels.

"I'll handle Nate, sir," Jeff promised.

"See that you do," Kels said, while he turned on his heel and walked back to his car, "Good luck out there," he added. They watched him drive off the tarmac. I saw Meg turn to look into her husband's eyes - the same way she had once looked into mine. Her dimples bearing the warm smile that she flashed at Jeff, "That's an order I guess," she said playfully at Kel's admonishment of *bon fortune*.

I remembered that playfulness. I knew it long before Jeff ever did and had purged it from my mind long before he had ever met her. Meg is someone who knew what being alive entails. One night we had just come back from a too crowded dance club. Me, I'm not one for crowds, but she loved it and I loved watching her move while she stared into my eyes - poetry in pumps. She had me guessing as if she was trying to learn something or decide something by gazing so intently. But we had both worked up quite a sweat. So much so that nothing more than a quick kiss on the cheek was expected after helping her unlock her door and see her inside. But she pulled back saying, "I'm sorry Nate, I really need a shower," flashing those dimples and heading across her apartment, unzipping and stepping out of her dress as she went. Reaching behind her back in one deft movement, she casually removed her brassier as she continued into the hall. She stood there before her open bathroom door, its light from behind her partially silhouetted her beguiling form. "Well," she said, letting her sheer lace panties fall around her heels, then nimbly skipping out of them, "are you coming?" The double entendre she intended wasn't lost on me. And I did, there in the shower while holding her smooth, shapely lathered hips from behind her - I'd pull her close against me, then I'd back away, pulling her tight, then backing away. "All I thought I was giving you was a peck on the cheek," I said afterwards. She straightened up and turned to me, and as I kissed her she breathlessly said, "And here I got your pecker."

Things were great. She began introducing me to family, then talking of our future. Having kids. Getting old together. Before you know it she's pregnant and your baby has a life threatening condition. They discover a cancer - hers. You wait and hope – wishing it were yours. And if it is you, you watch them watching you, waiting and hoping. The phone rings when your love isn't home and you get the call, "There's been a terrible accident. You need to come to the hospital immediately." Your heart has moved into your throat and you feel the color drain from your face as you watch the life drain from theirs. Death. Silence. Then the piercing howls from the macabre roll call of those left behind.

No, there will be none of that for me. Everyday, I ringmaster this circus of the damned, swimming against the vortex created by the whirlpool of emotions that will crush you like the pressure at the ocean's deepest floor. If I go down, no, it won't be by a hand that matters so dear, pulling me by my heart into that lost abyss.

It was some time after it was all over with Meg, that we bumped into each other again while Jeff was having black coffee with me. I introduced him to my 'acquaintance.' He fell hard. She once told him she had a silly crush on me, nothing more - it would serve nothing if she said more. I remember at their wedding, during the traditional garter toss, the groom slowly hiked up the bride's dress to comically tease the audience while he was about to remove the item. She flashed those dimples feigning embarrassment and tired of his prolongation, hiked her gown up well over the garter for him to find it, showing the side of her thigh - and the very edge of those same lace panties - ones I'd never see again, meeting my eye as if settling a long suppressed score.

Jeff looked on after Kels and his medical team troop inspection and told Meg, "He's just looking to move up to CEO."

"Here's another *order*," she said, "be careful, and keep a good eye on that big ape."

"That's no way to talk about poor Dengon," he said, rating a loving cuff upside his head from Meg who added, "Nate got us together remember?"

"You still love that big ape?"

"No, I *like* that big ape."

"Just remember who's your love monkey." He kissed her good-bye and climbed the aircraft's staircase as Mark followed.

Once inside the plane, Jeff stumbled back knocking Mark almost backward down the stairs when he saw me reclining in my seat. It was the best gorilla costume the party shop had for rent, though it was slightly itchy. "What?" I asked flippantly, "I wanted to go native. Guerillas. Blend in?" The gorilla head did make it slightly difficult to see but I could tell they weren't impressed. The rental cost was obviously worth it.

Though they tried to ignore me as they passed to their seats, I thought it important to share, "Bite my banana?" I offered of the remaining fruit bunch that rested suggestively erect in my lap.

"A kangaroo would've been the better costume choice," came the voice from the hatchway – it was Sierra. "At least you'd have a pouch for your junk," she added, referring to my micro-tablet data assistant that she flipped to me. Personal data assistants are a doctor's electronic peripheral brain. We can't, nor do we, 'know it all.' I didn't even know I forgot it at the nurse's station.

"Why don't you come along?" I teased, "It'd be nice to have someone to monkey around with in the untamed jungle. You'd get a life."

"Why don't you get a wife?" she instructed.

"Owww. Geez Sierra, you don't have to use profanity," I answered while I clutched my torso - direct hit. Her words struck me where I suppose my heart would be - if I really had ever grown one. I watched her go while the ground crew sealed the door and the plane taxied to the runway.

She walked off the tarmac with a peaceful, confident stride like that of the tarmac marshals, who guide the planes in and out with those light sticks they wave, who are satisfied to have seen their 'bird' off, but don't care to ever fly the plane. She could though. She could fly. For she and her walk belonged in whatever moment they were in. Lucky lady.

SUPPLEMENTAL ENTRY

I don't know how long I was asleep. Seemed like days. The drone of the engines and the sheer fatigue of recent events had taken their toll. I awoke and looked outside the plane's window. I took off the sweaty, smelly gorilla head for a better look. I could see exotic birds darting in and out of the distant jungle canopy below. They flew fast. Some were too fast to make out what they were, and some appeared too small, yet fast enough to know their identity exactly.

"Tracer fire? *Nobody* said anything about tracer fire."

"Relax," Jeff told me, "we're outta range."

Rebels and guerillas are always skirmishing with the government, I was told. Why people would fight over a country with one of the poorest populations and that likely has only one Facebook account for several million people to share, I'll never know. Until, that is, Dengon reminded me that it is considered one of the richest areas on the Earth in terms of its untapped mineral resources. No hospitals or trauma bays down there I'm sure. Any serious injury and the medical treatment would consist of TAP - Tourniquet, Amputate, or Put-em-down.

Having stripped off the rest of the gorilla suit, I felt the gentle jolt of the landing gear swing down and lock beneath the fuselage. The landing on one of the only paved runways in the country was surprisingly smooth. So was the taxiway to the dilapidated, corrugated, sheet metal Quonset hut that served as terminal. Smooth, customs wasn't.

Agents, who were more like freelance rent-a-cops, swarmed the plane asking for passports, ID, and quietly of course, cash. Turfle and Henley showed them papers proving that we were on a chartered medical mission. But upon eyeing the expensive gear and research swag being offloaded from the plane's belly, well, this dump likely doesn't get much in the way of opportunity. Henley went into the terminal with one agent as Turfle opened equipment bags for the other who tried to keep the barrel of his shoulder-slung AK-47 from bumping into what Turfle offered for his inspection. I nervously watched, hoping that he didn't see my medical bag. I don't remember the research paperwork specifically listing the controlled substances or narcotics that I had in my bag. If they wanted to push the issue we - or specifically, I - could be looking at being here until the local prison rodent population had groomed their paws after feasting on my corpse. I tried to think up some diversion, as he got closer to finding my bag with its jump kit, just as Henley emerged from the terminal Quonset, wiping lipstick from his collar, "Geez, I can't believe what a whore costs down here."

"Where's the Customs Officer?" Jeff asked.

"Locked in his office getting his rocks off, courtesy of our research grant." At which the inspecting officer hurriedly snatched the duty fees - payola - for our imported equipment from Turfle's hand and rushed off to presumably get a little snatch of his own.

"You didn't," I asked, referring to the smeared flaming red grease paint he still worked to remove from his collar.

"Naw, she just thought I was the john at first when she saw the cash. First airport I been to where Customs is just as happy to stamp some *behind*, rather than your passport."

Dengon observed, "Women in these parts always look for a flyboy to take them out of here, if no lonely flyboy, cash will do."

Dengon had already procured our transportation. A look at the two mud encrusted, rusty jeeps, and an ancient busted up half Land Rover, half several other vehicles cobbled together, and one would wonder if they missed the memo that those models powered by a mangy mongoose on a hamster wheel were recalled a stone age ago. The extensive corrosion spots pockmarked the vehicles throughout their sheet metal body, some of which went all the way through the undercarriage. On the latter vehicle, by the dents and broken headlight, one would not be far off to surmise that they must have used tow chains and beat the ferrous beast mercilessly to get it to come to rest in its current parking space. The seats wore a metal frame with a crisscross pattern of nylon straps forming the back and tush rest. Rough ride. "The kidney cruncher special," I mumble.

Dengon only beamed at the rolling deathtraps however, "They reserved their best ones for us. This is very good," he commented with all seriousness. I really didn't care what they looked like. I figured that at least being on the move we'd avoid continuing as the strolling bug buffet - the biting flies and mosquitoes were so big, they surely required runway clearance from the airport. They were fast, too. A mosquito I attempted to swat was so quick; it moved faster than my Internet bandwidth at home. It continued to buzz me like a bully, teasing its victim before it sucked the life out. However, as I was already in this godforsaken no-man's land, I decided to go native and ate the little bastard. One bite. Mid-air. No real taste but his protein was mine now. Could it be that the loony bed wasn't such a bad idea after all?

ENTRY 4

Insects have a rather nutty taste. Guess it's, 'eat or be eaten.' Jungle rule. Same as the city rule – come to think about it. Damn, I've been around too much pain and suffering.

I tried to shower in the pungent mist of bug repellant while we drove down what barely resembles a road. I manage to spray my eyes, my mouth and the humid tropical air - everywhere but where I wanted, mistiming nozzle squirts with the crater strikes by our wheels on the road. The vehicles now miserably resplendent in their new coat of dusty road grime bumped and rocked over the trail. The new filth was much more uniform than the old coat of grime and this Congo bondo - or dried African mud - held the rattling fenders to their chassis attachments just enough to make you wonder if they were trying to decide whether to hang on for added punishment or depart the rusted hulks.

Jeff didn't seem to mind the adventure, "Just like the potholes back home, eh Nate?"

I craned my neck to look out over the side of the jeep and study the vintage wheels, "Would've sworn that they were square," I noted, at how unbalanced and unsafe they looked. "We'll have to turn back if they take one more - ," BANG! A banyan-like tree's roots exploded and flipped our jeep onto its side. We spilled into the Congo-an dust, dazed and disordered. When I opened my eyes, I didn't know which end was up but saw the big banyan tree slowly toppling over from the blast. I felt Jeff's stilled body against my leg and with my foot, shoved him to roll down the edge of the shallow ravine near us and out of the timber's imminent path. A series of snaps and crunches broke the momentary silence as the giant old leafy thing now divorced from what roots had remained, left me barely time to roll out of its deadly trajectory.

Yet, even after the old wood now rested on the ground, there were more bursts. Gunfire! Ragtag guerrilla fighters appeared from out of the bushes and yelled at us in a language we didn't understand. But the barrels of their guns stuck in our faces were a dialect we all understood and validated their compadres credit authorization to rummage through our stuff.

"Potholes, carjacking, hey, you guys got an American Coney Island around here?" I asked. It was almost like home. I didn't concern myself that I'd put my foot in my mouth; one of the guerillas did it for me - hard. I mused, "Must be a Lafayette Coney man," after I spit out blood mixed with the soil off the toe of his boot. If we lived through this and got back to

Detroit, I'd show any rescuers where to find the American and Lafayette Coney Island shops right next-door to each other - each with fiercely loyal customers. A loosened tooth clued me in that carryout wasn't an option right now.

Other armed guerillas herded the rest of the caravan's occupants over to where we were sprawled out with encouragement from the tips of their rifles. Slowly, Jeff and I began to regain our senses and one of the first things I noticed was Dengon and my read on him. The sides of his cheeks moved slightly - expanding and flattening – as he clenched his teeth while keenly observing the rebels. We were all nervous. He was panicked. That told me things were about to get worse.

One guerilla rummaged through the medical supplies then got into Henley's face, "Clap trap, clap trap," he said in broken English while pointing to his crotch. "Fix."

Henley as an administrator was clueless, but obviously the terrorist wanted antibiotics for a chlamydia infection, or some kind of sexually transmitted disease that he had. Made me wonder if he'd been to the local airport recently.

Turfle wasn't the least bit phased, his mind on the mission, "As long as they leave the lab gear..." his voice was interrupted by a loud CRASH from the rear of the jeep. "...intact," his sentence now finished, as was some expensive gear. By now it was a free for all with other rebels feasting on our food supplies and sending some of it back into the bush with their comrades.

Two other rebels standing guard over us then winked at each other and racked a shell round into the firing chamber of their guns. One rebel next leveled the barrel behind Mark's ear.

Mark sweat even more than before, "That's a s-sausage grinder," he stuttered in reference to the machine gun's tip, "N-no coney's," then he urinated himself.

"Guess we're not their table," I answered wondering whether I should at least try for a quick hit to their balls. Just something to remember me by and keep my mind focused to avoid pissing myself, at least until after they shoot me dead. It is a fairly common occurrence when you die, you know. Too many times I've seen it in the ER when shooting victims come in dead and the corpse already had evacuated its bowels and bladder. It's as if the body gives one last attempt at self-survival by releasing its most offensive elements as perhaps some primitive way to make whatever was threatening it flee and leave it alone. A primitive response to the most primitive of actions: senseless violence. It always amazed me in the trauma bays how many times its purveyors foolishly believed they'd win through inflicting this violence upon their victim, when in reality, they are the ones it ultimately consumes - one way or another.

Then, there was echoed laughter – 'the best medicine.' And for us, it was. It echoed from our Land Rover and with it, the rebels' kill shots were stayed. The guards had paused to watch a comrade hold aloft a zebra skin design bra and panties - couldn't keep their guns level if they wanted to from the guffaws and chortles.

"Those don't look like test tubes," I murmured.

Jeff was a shade redder than from just the jungle sun, as he announced to the inquisitively gun prodding guards, "They're mine." Embarrassed, Jeff tapped his chest with both hands to demonstrate possession and added, "From the airport when we landed. For my wife." This latter sentence he added, no doubt, due to the rising mirth from the guards at the mental picture of the big hairy man in Chantilly lace bra and peek-a-boo panties. We didn't understand at first why, a big and fat guerrilla grabbing the find rushed over and waved it at us as if to determine whose it was. Perhaps they didn't understand what Jeff had said. We all pointed to poor Jeff, asserting as one, "They're his!"

"Ho-kay" said the guerilla finally in broken English, "we kill all you first, and your friend we allow to live to get pretty before he dies," there was more laughter as they motioned to force Jeff to move closer to don the undergarments. Their rifle barrels once again were leveled at the rest of us to finish the job.

The first bullet punched a hole through the seat of the zebra drawers that were still held aloft, and ricocheted off the overturned jeep. The guerillas were confused at this for but a second, for a maelstrom of copper jacketed lead death, quickly followed that single shot and they took up positions. Being unarmed, we were quickly forgotten and left to ourselves as the guerrillas ducked behind the wreckage and returned fire.

More government troops now took up positions behind boulders and trees and continued the firefight. We crawled along the ground. Our parched lips were made all the more dry by the dust that caked to them while rounds of ammo whizzed above our heads as we attempted to get back to the Land Rover and single Jeep that still had its rubber on the road. I spotted my medical bag a few feet away and reached to my side for it, while I continued making like a hermit crab on the ground. The bag was stuck. Stuck because a guerilla on the ground had also made claim to it with his foot planted on the handle as it lay on its side. "I don't have time to argue," I argued, as a large section of freshly wounded branches crashed down onto the disputed medical bag. My hand throbbed in pain from the crushing blow of the wood, making me flop like some comical fish out of water. It brought the guerilla a few moments of mirth judging by the smile upon his dirty unshaved face. "You don't time to argue," he said in a mocking tone as he mimicked me.

"And neither do you," I replied at the sight of the large gray-green intruder that reared up. The Black Mamba was obviously very hissed off - hey, snakes don't piss - at having been disturbed from its treetop-resting place and brought into the noisy atmosphere. As the man reached down for the bag, it struck. Its fangs pierced the guerilla's face before it struck again, this time at his eye. It proved what I had known about their repeated strikes injecting large amounts of venom. His smile now gone, he jumped up and hopped around in pain before being felled by the cardio-neurotoxin. The dropped bag, now back in my possession, accompanied my own slithering back to the vehicles.

The rest of the group wasn't waiting for me. With gears engaged, they lurched ahead, the Land Rover not stopping enough for me to jump in, and the remaining Jeep, only slowing because of the Land Rover it followed. But it was enough for me to have grabbed onto the spare tire on the well-rusted tailgate. The Jeep sped forward like an animal having its tail nipped. My added weight broke the rusted supports on the tailgate. It flipped down - the ground rushed by beneath me in a steady unending blur - until Dengon hit the brakes. The sudden deceleration caused the tailgate to flip up and slam shut. At this, I was hurled up and over the gate into the backseat, my legs sticking up like a two-buck Cass Corridor hooker advertising a sale.

"Don't do that, Doctor, sir," Dengon yelled, looking over his shoulder while he still managed to somehow drive the narrow road, "that's a rude gesture to some tribes."

"I've got another one for you," I shot back.

ENTRY 5

We were far enough away from any civilization now, that risking my life for the medical bag seemed like a stupid idea. If anything was to go wrong, there'd be no nearby hospital, no way to call for an airlift chopper, no ambulance. The bag might help fix some minor wounds or stabilize some malady or injury for a few hours, but ultimately, it would only prolong the inevitable - *death.* When you're in my business, you think about it a lot. ***The inevitable.*** If we were to strip away the titles before our name or the initials after it and any remora-like hubris, we *are* the great pretenders. We 'guardians of life' and first responders, privately congratulate ourselves for every 'save,' even when everyone else forgets to or never bothers. But it's not so much a save as a 'stay' of sentencing. *You have been rescued from dying today, but just how will you die tomorrow?* Would all human accomplishment wither from the existence if this morbid fact was focused on? Or, in seeing the mortal face of others reflected in that of our own, would we all strive for even loftier achievements, closer kinships and love? Come *it* will, however, and I've asked myself, 'how many of us who have experienced this, really would change the way we live our lives because of this awareness?' Some would undoubtedly change for the better. But how many others would despair and give up? And which, really, have I cast my lot with?

A foggy notion formed in my stress-addled brain, like the low clouds that approached from over the desert in the distance, "Now's a good time to go back," I said, while I slapped at yet another new species of tiny biting insect. I marveled that these winged warriors would manage to keep up, reasoning that they must be biting due to a coming change in the weather. I began to believe that trying to find a primitive native group on the roam would most likely be fruitless - it's a big continent. Jeff would have none of it and thus, onward we continued.

Storm clouds rolled in fast over the changing terrain - faster than I had ever seen before. Dengon gripped the wheel all the tighter, "Haboob," he said as he stepped on the gas pedal hard, "Dust storm." At just a few hundred feet change in elevation, one would begin to see the vegetation change - dry in the lower lands and jungle in the higher.

"Now's even a better time to go back," I repeated to Jeff's annoyance.

"He may be right," agreed Dengon.

There would be no outrunning it. We fumbled around with goggles to protect our eyes and hastily tied bandanas around our noses and mouths to keep out the wind whipped, choking sand. In just that time, it swallowed us. We could barely see or hear. There was dust everywhere, like an otherworldly state of matter, one which was both solid and liquid, and yet neither.

"We need to slow down," I shouted above the wind.

Dengon tried to reassure me, "I know these roads." A fact that I conceded since he was the guide, and in short time, despite the flying dirt, we were gently rocking down the road where we had bounced just moments ago.

"Why is the road suddenly bobbing?" asked Jeff. He received his answer when the raging dust storm cleared just enough to see that we had been swept up in the path of a mudslide – one that had become its own class 5 rapids. Cascading around us, it swept us along quickly with other debris. This primeval ooze was dark and cold and encasing. If lava had a poor bastard stepchild, this would be it. We could hear thunder in the distance. The rush of the outlying storm runoff, unable to be absorbed by the rock hills beyond, mixed with dirt to become even more of a torrential ooze.

The fender of the our jeep crumpled as it was slammed into the quarter panel of the Land Rover by the wave of mud that used us the way a tempestuous child rolls one toy car into another for the satisfaction of knowing he has the control to ordain it so. Mud flowed into the sides of the open jeep's occupant compartment to come and finally claim us. It covered our feet and ankles, like a liquid python sensing and entwining its prey before the kill. Swimming would be useless, if not outright suicide. The ooze continued to swallow the jeep. Instinctively we stood up and the jeep sunk deeper as it was swept along. The only chance was to grab the luggage rail on the nearby Rover's roof. No small feat as one moment it bumped us, and then in the next it was carried a few feet apart from us. Before I could call it out, Dengon knew a jump to the other vehicle was the only chance, even if it would be only prolonging the inevitable. He jumped and I slipped. He caught hold of the luggage rail - I caught his belt.

Never, *ever* hang your fate by a skinny-assed native guide with no butt. His pants were slipping like a last year politician's approval rating. Of all the times to go commando - his odiferous butt crack rose from the lowering belt line like a perverse vertical grin mocking me to my unfortunate face. It was only from my anger that I was able to give one last tug as I yanked myself up and threw my hand up and grasped the rail above. What pants loosely remained around Dengon's legs, were sucked off by the ooze and disappeared into the muck.

Hanging on for life itself, we were flung back and forth like those swaying mechanical carwash rag-ribbons against the side windows of the Land Rover. I laughed a nervous laugh, for while we bobbed to and fro, the poor Rover's occupants were treated to the unenviable view of Dengon's privates swaying against the window like a windshield wiper from hell.

Our metamorphosed, four-wheeled amphibian spun around a little before failing to negotiate a sudden turn that the swift mudslide decided to take. It was there that the ooze seemed to be tired of its toy when it hurled the Rover and crew between two closely grown tree trunks. There, on a bank, the Rover was well wedged as mud slogged over us and the others scrambled to get out of the vehicle. They anxiously grasped for land lest the erosive action of the voracious river of mud took over and sweep away the trees by their now exposed roots.

Dengon and I had been tossed forward onto solid ground from the impact. The mud was now cold but at least it kept the biting insects away and cooled my sunburnt skin. My pants-less fellow sludge monster drew the muck away from his eyes with his hands and surveyed the land, "We're here."

"Where's 'here,'?" Jeff asked Dengon.

"Nowhere," I muttered, as we were in *deep*, going from 'bad' to 'hopeless.'

"Ah, safe," proclaimed Dr. Turffle, like an old hand that had ridden this rodeo before. He had even managed to grab a pair of shorts before exiting the vehicle to toss over for Dengon to regain his dignity.

Dengon still dripped with mud as he parted the bushes to share his find with us. Beyond the divided bush in the distance, we saw a Congoan village of a few mud huts with thatched grass roofs. Most structures, however, were crudely thatched shelters and lean-tos of nomadic peoples.

An arrow ripped through Turffle's jungle hat. Raising his eyes upward as if to look, the color drained from his face. I waited for a crimson stream to flow down his forehead. But no blood drained from a wound to his head - the hat was the only casualty.

I glared at Turffle and mockingly said, "Safe,' you say?"

The brush and its branches began to move unnaturally as arms sprouted and opposable thumbs germinated from their dense green leaves. The very vegetation came to life around us embodied with several Bushmen who had sprung forth, right in front of us. So well camouflaged were they that they were close enough to kill us without any prior warning if they so chose.

We were herded into the village at spear point, while the mosquitoes stabbed any non-muddied body area with their hungry proboscises. Dengon talked quickly in their native tongue – no doubt trying to explain our purpose and avoid being skewered - but the guard only answered with the gentle jab of the point of his primitive spear to keep him moving. Dengon reached into his shirt pocket and withdrew a chocolate bar. Without turning around to face the spear bearer, he held it aloft above his shoulder to catch the eye of that intimidating guard behind him. It was more an instant fondue kit in a wrapper from the heat, since the now liquefied bar's sweet goo all settled in the bottom of the wrapper. Chocolate. Go figure its therapeutic power - soothes a woman's jilted heart and tames a savage warrior.

"What about Goliath?" Jeff inquired, sensing a moment to continue the quest, "Is it the right village?"

The guard's verbal exchange with Dengon was a little friendlier this time, though still wary, as he sucked the sweet brown confection from the wrapper.

"It's the right one," Dengon replied, "he says it came here with an Asian zoo expedition and was chased away."

There was at once, a sound of a million cicadas that emanated from the treetops from every direction. Only it had an increasingly rhythmic pitch and was building to a frenzied crescendo as if determined to split our very skulls.

Rattles. Rattles of something made by someone unseen.

Bellowing over the din, Jeff persisted, "Where did they get the cure?"

The native mumbled something to Dengon and pointed skyward.

"He said to, 'look up,'" Dengon replied.

We all looked up, the cicada sound grew even louder. The trees themselves even seemed to reverberate with the eerie mesmerizing sound. A little louder and we would have missed the soft *thump* from the pair of feet that planted squarely on the ground behind us. We quickly turned to confront whoever it was that landed his or her jump, but nobody was there. As I looked up, I thought I saw the bottom of a man's foot, possibly a native, rocket up into the lush vine laced canopy above. But one shadow among the canopy leaves seemed to become lost with another as the wind played among the branches.

The breeze also played with the exotic flowered necklace that hung from the neck of a most beautiful young native woman whom I noticed to have appeared in the distance. The petals danced all the more over her chest as she giggled at our puzzlement. Her smile was infectious and beautiful - a surprise to me since it was likely that there wasn't a dentist to be found for maybe a thousand miles or so - and I slowly approached her side. The flowers of the necklace were like a variation of the type whose parts are used by druggies as a hallucinogen. Getting a closer look, her smile still beckoned and I gently reached up to finger the petals that were as silky as her bronzed skin. The hums of the cicada sound now almost a dreamy serenade.

There was a sound like a whisper. Not of her lips, but of the wind and for but an instant - an arrow flew to my heart! A *real*, stone tipped, wooden shafted, feather tailed - freaking ARROW! It appeared as if from nowhere and it remained there, that chiseled arrowhead, frozen an inch or two from my throat, its shaft in the tight fist of the one they called, Bakuya Muntabbi. He appeared as suddenly as the arrow from out of the jungle canopy above. The cicada sounds had now all fallen silent. It was as if the very jungle stilled its air.

This man who held the arrow fast in his grip and stayed my execution narrowed his eyes upon me. He wrinkled his brow and twitched his nose rather annoyed, creasing the bizarre berry juice icons that adorned his face. What they may have represented I couldn't begin to guess and didn't want to know. Upon his arms were decorative keloids. These were really just scars - a form of primitive tattoo that no laser could remove later if one tired of them. He wore a breastplate of small colored twigs horizontally woven together in a tight ordered fashion. His pants, or more like the shredded remains of what was left of them, still bore the partial remains of the logo from their original maker - " ockers." Except for him, the entire native group wore leaf festooned loincloths, even the angry native who held the deadly bow and reached for another round from his quiver.

The native who had saved me walked with a swagger of authority back toward the armed archer who still cast his angry, jealous glare at me. Dengon informed me that the arrow catcher was "the witch doctor" of the tribe. He bent forward to whisper this to keep his distance from me lest he become a consolation prize for any errant in-flight arrows. The good 'doctor' handed the captured arrow back to his tribesman while he spoke in what was his native tongue. I later learned he told this tribal warrior, "If the strangers are harmed, more may come." The young warrior looked away in disgust. How was I to know his bride was a flirt?

But the rest of the villagers took notice only of their esteemed witch doctor in their presence. A couple of native men fastened a cloak over his shoulders while several native girls laid leaves before him as he walked. A nightmarish headdress festooned with multiple protruding horns and exotic feathers was placed upon his head. The rest of the villagers parted to make way for him to ascend his ceremonial throne. The rest of the team and I all gasped as he sat and this obviously pleased him - for he took it as a sign of awe and respect of his position. The gasp was of his position all right, right atop the sharp points of rows of rusty spikes that made up the seat of the chair. He sat there without a grimace, without so much as a twitch. The back of the chair was of discarded barbed wire that had bones woven throughout it. The armrests were the preserved decapitated heads of crocodiles, their toothy mouths fixed wide open. The witch doctor asked in his native language, "Does any man among you speak my tongue?"

Dengon hurried over to the throne and told him that he was indeed our translator. The witch doctor carefully studied this mouthpiece guide who stood before him for a good moment or two. Dengon then translated the following for the rest of us, as the witch doctor spoke, "He says we're unwelcome outsiders and we are asked to leave immediately by decree of Grand Tribal Healer, Bakuya Muntabbi."

Mark however, still hadn't made the course correction and answered, "Tell him that we've come a long way and that our vehicles are stuck or lost," which Dengon did as per the request. Muntabbi raised his hand up in a silent command and several burly natives came forward pulling hard on the heavy ropes as they towed the two muddied vehicles into camp by their bumpers.

"'Problem solved,' he said," parroted Dengon of the witch doctor.

While the guys huddled to discuss their next move, I felt left alone as the human sacrifice to the tiny bugs that had once again zeroed in on my exposed areas of flesh. I slapped at them every which way to the amusement of the locals. I was too busy slapping myself and thinking of the various pathogens likely checking into my body, courtesy of the biting, buzzing little vectors, to have initially been aware of the witch doctor. He pointed to me while asking Dengon, "What's his problem?"

"Gnats," translated Dengon, as Jeff broke from the huddle and said, "Tell him we need to talk to his Witchdoctorship to learn the cure for Goliath."

Dengon again mediated for the now perturbed medicine man, "The witch doctor says all of you, 'should first learn that a poison dart cannot be stopped as easily as the arrow.'" To make his point, he motioned to that jealous young warrior groom off to the side, who now held a blowgun instead of his bow and grinned at me, a grin that let me know this tribesman was just itching to pin-the-dart-on-the-doctor.

Mark, however, was focused, like a kid who continued to whine for that new gaming console despite being told his parents just lost the family home in which to keep it, "Please, we've come a long way," he said.

"He's a fake," I shouted, barely able to contain my momentary mirth at the thought of this hand wringing over a savage. I couldn't stand it anymore. The *begging* before a primitive that wouldn't know an enema suppository from a cough drop was just too much. His eyes were upon me and narrowed. He understood my interruption as a lack of respect, even if not my words, which spewed forth like a frenzied machine gun, "I've been bug bait since we got here. I've been shot at. I've got rashes in places that should be reported to the health department." A glop of mud slid down my forehead that I wiped away with the back of my hand and slung down at Muntabbi's feet. Some of the tribe trembled at that while I added, "You actually *think* that this *whack job* with a turkey ass on his head - look at *all* those feathers - is gonna cure anything?"

I decided that *I* was going to plant my ass in that muddied jeep - even if the others wanted to make fools of themselves - and I wasn't going to budge from the seat until it was parked at the airport for the flight home. I stepped confidently away towards the jeep but only managed to boldly trample my dignity by stepping in "Goat dung!" It was with great disgust that I wiped the smashed pile of squished, posterior pellets from my shoe and kicked it onto the area opposite that weird porta-throne.

Dengon rolled his eyes, at which I yelled, "Dung! I can get dung at home. Free! Lots of it!" Another bug fell upon my shoulder from the trees causing me to wonder its species. "Dung beetle," Dengon casually informed.

Muntabbi had jumped up from his seat and pointed at me with his bizarre rattle-scepter-thing-a-ma-bobby, shouting gibberish at my outburst. Whatever he was now saying was almost too much for Dengon to process as he rapidly tried to keep up and translated, "The witch doctor says you have defiled the ground in the path of the throne which is sacred. He must now perform the cleansing ritual."

As if to mimick the grip the witch doctor had around the rattle, Jeff's fingers tightened around my shoulder and gently shook me while he whispered into my ear, "You're blowing it, former buddy."

"There's nothing here to 'blow'," I added while I shook his grip free.

A young village boy wasn't able to do likewise from his mother's grip. The child shrieked like a blasted siren when she yanked him by his arm to pull him to what she supposed was her safety, from the unfolding events. A well-meaning mother who didn't know what she had really done. The little boy's sobs yielded their decibel dominance to the beat of animal skin drums and percussion instruments. The infernal noise of the rattle grew in volume. It choreographed each step of the witch doctor that led from his esteemed throne of rubbish to the ground, where he began an elaborate ritual tribal dance.

It was a rather interesting dance, with arms and legs flailing this way and that. He moved across the compound then paused before me - the irreverent intruder, who mimicked his roaring tiger mouth impression mid roar with a gaping yawn of my own. Oh, he was in his glory hopping around until he looked back and saw me awkwardly dancing too. I copied a few of his arm thrusts and leg swings and added a few Detroit style club moves of my own that were really more like focal motor seizures. He executed some flips and twirls clearly for dominance sake, to affirm HE was the doctor - and it was *on*. I never did any break dancing but wasn't shy - a twist here, a jump and turn there and a popped disc in my lower back down there -

shit - and his native minions were impressed. Even Blow-Gun-Bob, who fancied my loins roasting over the campfire for ogling his bride's goodies, grinned – either that, or he was pleased that I now similarly vexed the one who had saved this intruder from his arrow's wrath. It was 'dueling banjos' within a dance set.

He wasn't the most considerate partner however, as with a well-timed sweep of his legs, he knocked mine right out from underneath me. Down I went into, yep, goat dung. He finished his dance rather triumphantly over my stunned body and glared at me with a final smugness. The villagers clamored around him like he was a deity, while I worked to upright my sore back and limped over to the huddled unwelcome party of my fellow exiles.

"I agree with Jeff," said Mark, "you need to apologize."

I rubbed my back as I said, "I save lives and I'm locked up in a loony bin. He dances and he's a god."

"His dancing's better," Jeff remarked.

A native stumbled out from behind the back of our jeep. Obviously mocking my dance steps as well, I had thought - until I noticed that he held an empty aftershave bottle he apparently lifted from one of the guys' bags. By his aromatic odor, he had rubbed it on, by his breath he had drank it and by the large welts he vigorously scratched at, he was reacting to it. His eyes were almost swollen shut and he began to clutch at his throat sounding like he was drowning.

Jeff only uttered, "Wha -"

" - Anaphylaxis," I said.

I was informed at this point that the witch doctor called for his rattles and pouch, but I was already at the jeep looking for the medical bag and the villagers were looking in their quivers for arrows while Blow-Gun-Bob eagerly loaded another round. The witch doctor got to him first and shook his rattles and incanted, "Hanah-ub-keeli-hanah-bo-tini. Hanah-ub-keeli-hanah-bo-tini," as some of the villagers joined him.

There, wedged beneath the seat and thus keeping itself from being swept away in the flood-o-filth, was the muddied medical kit. I ran back to the stricken native who was turning a lovely shade of, well, it was hard to tell just what shade he was turning with his coating of body paints, but a little more time and it wouldn't have mattered. I'd never get through the native guard that sought to keep us away.

Rather than stop my run toward the tribal patient, I slid in the dirt like the Detroit Tiger's first baseman, right between and underneath the spread legs of a native guard, the witch doctor and, a young woman assisting the witch doctor - no time to be disgusted by, nor admire the views above the path of my slide. I whipped out the Epinephrine autoinjector and jammed it into the anterior thigh of the stricken aftershave thief. With a *click* the epinephrine medicine was delivered beneath his skin.

Dengon translated the angry festooned leader's words, "The witch doctor said for you to move away from his patient, Nate."

"When I'm done," I replied, while trying to avoid eye contact with the savage's burning evil orbs that glared at me, and instead, focused on filling a syringe from a vial marked *diphenhydramine*. The witch doctor tightened his masticator muscles beneath the skin of the sides of his cheeks by grinding his teeth together at my refusal to yield and menacingly snatched a spear from the hands of a fellow savage. I had just enough time to inject the second drug before standing up to defiantly face the witch doctor, eye to eye.

"Done," I said without a blink.

The witch doctor had a lot to say too - whatever it was. I don't know what it exactly was, but native women covered the ears of their children.

"Forget the magic elixir," I grumbled, "They're not giving us anything." I smacked the umpteenth mosquito as I headed back for the jeep. "A fraud has nothing to give," I added.

I wondered as I walked, if at any moment now, I would feel the spear's piercing point, the poison dart's sting, the stab of the arrowhead or all of them at once. The witch doctor was so focused on his diatribe against me, that he didn't pay attention to the aftershave guzzler who stood up behind him, with his eyes noticeably less swollen, his hives almost gone.

The witch doctor grew more irate as I noticed the villagers stare at the improving native who moved among them, then at me, then at the witch doctor. The rest of the team packed up to leave. The mission had officially failed. They were unimpressed with our request and perhaps our medicine. Only Dr. Turffle's muttering broke the now silent jungle, "Nothing. All this way. For nothing."

"You didn't help things much, Nate," Mark added, throttling one of the bags to fit into the remaining vehicles and probably imagining it was my neck.

Muntabbi looked over "our" patient, before he surprisingly - not understanding English - seemed to puzzle over what I said next.

"Practicing here's about as thankless as practicing back home these days."

The witch doctor continued to keenly observe and listen when Dengon interpreted, "We leave you now in peace," he said towards the lead savage on our behalf.

It would only be later, on the plane home, that Dengon told me what Muntabbi said in bewilderment to Blow-Gun-Bob, who had hoped for permission to take one final shot at me before we left - "His medicine is strong, yet *he* is afflicted." But the young warriors sternly shook their spears and weapons to encourage our team to be quickly off on our departure.

I was very glad to be leaving and as I piled into the vehicle with the rest of the crew, it was then that I noticed that small, young, village boy still whimpering and favoring his arm that had been yanked.

Dengon put the key in the ignition and turned the engine over as Jeff observed, "With those spear tips doubling in number, for once I agree, it's time to go."

"Hold it," I said, and stepped out of the vehicle, "I'm *not* done yet." As I said this, Muntabbi confronted me eye to eye for but a moment. I wouldn't yield, would he? Or would he have me killed in cold blood and serve me in a nice hollandaise sauce? Yet, again, he kept my hide intact when he put his arm out to stay the spear tip one of his warriors brandished at me. I crossed over to the young boy who now looked up at me. Fear flashed from his eyes and nervous curiosity commandeered his face. He would never know fear of a white coat though. Nor the anxiety brought on by the sight of an immunization needle, nor the protections they afforded. His life could be cut short by a wild animal attack or any manner of infections that would overtake his body without antibiotics - medicine that those back home take for granted. An accidental injury could render him permanently crippled or disfigured in his world, where it would only be a temporary annoyance or a simple scar in ours. Weakness in this land could lead one to go from hunter to prey.

I gently took his wrist in my hand and felt his muscles tighten in apprehension, while I put the thumb of my other hand over the radial head of his elbow – that little bump there on the outside of the elbow. With a gentle flexing of his forearm at the elbow while pushing with my thumb and rotating his wrist inwardly, I felt the small 'pop' that let me know my efforts had succeeded. I walked back to the jeep and the boy ran to his father and waved his fixed appendage vigorously at the witch doctor.

"He's showing his arm works again .,.to his father," called Dengon.

"Some shaman," I answered, directed more to Muntabbi's ear than at Dengon's, "can't even help his own child with a simple Nursemaid's Elbow." I settled in and Dengon edged us onto the semblance of road that would hopefully take us home.

"Wait!" called Muntabbi in perfectly understandable English, "Are you not afraid of death?" Everything and everyone abruptly stopped, and for a moment it seemed, so did the current epoch itself.

"It's the living that I find hard sometimes," I answered.

"English?" inquired Jeff, "He speaks English?"

"I, Bakuya Muntabbi, is no fraud."

Well, almost perfectly understandable English.

"A con man too," I commented.

"Where did you learn to speak English?" asked Dengon no longer translating.

"Missionaries who came into the jungle."

"You allow outsiders in after all?" quizzed Mark.

"Only for them to pass," Muntabbi replied with a loud *burp,* "Good cook. The English teacher was most tasty." At this cannibalistic revelation, it looked like Mark and Jeff were about to pass something in *their* pants.

"You have come to seek Muntabbi's medicine for the illness brought by the animal catchers," Muntabbi continued.

"The zoo team, yes," affirmed Dr. Turffle.

"Our organization will be most grateful," Jeff chimed in.

Mark acted like a kid who suddenly discovered his gift under the Christmas tree and added, "You'll share the elixir with us then?"

"No," said Muntabbi.

"No?" echoed Dr. Turffle.

"But with *him*," Muntabbi added while he pointed at me, "Only if I can go observe his secrets of medicine. From where do you come?"

"United States," said Jeff.

"The Wolverine State," I added condescendingly.

At this, Muntabbi turned back towards the villagers and in native tongue said, "My people, I must go with these men." There was a somber mumbling of discontent that rippled through the village. Muntabbi's older son and protégé, who was in his late teens or early twenties, stepped forward from the crowd with that 'gazelle in the headlights' look. Muntabbi continued, "I leave my apprentice, my son, in my absence.

"Father, no. I am not ready," his son stressed, "You know what will happen --"

"-- You will be ready," Muntabbi reassured, "Besides, it is written long ago of a great magic that comes from wolverine urine."

"If I fail father, we could be banished."

"Don't fail," Muntabbi grinned, and gave the worried lad a good-natured nudge and blowing his nose in his hands, wiped them on top of the boy's head in a blessing. He then turned his attention to me, while he proclaimed to our team, "After I have lived with this man to determine his worthiness, you will know of the magic of Muntabbi." His hand pounced on my shoulder like a powerful bear's claw, surprising me with his strength for someone in his early fifties, "You may call me 'Bakuya'."

Then his words hit me, "Lived with?" I echoed through clenched teeth.

"His name is Nate," Jeff added, now running with the ball.

"Gnat," Bakuya said.

"Nate," I corrected, and slapped another biting insect on my upper arm. Bakuya mimicked this action and said, "Yes, I know. Gnat. And I look forward to seeing the wolverine, as well." Before I could protest any further Jeff pulled me aside and whispered into my ear.

"One word there are no wolverines in Michigan, *Gnat*, and hospital administration will have your kahunas stuffed and buttered as an appetizer at their next board meeting."

"I don't do *roomies* with cannibals," I shot back, although too late, for Mark had already closed the deal and crowed, "We're all agreed then?" The rest were eager to sell me out and nodded their approval and Bakuya hurried into his hut.

"The land of democracy is *across* the ocean, *not here*," I protested at being outvoted, "It's *my* life –"

"- Okay," Jeff broke in, "we've been friends a long time, Nate and -"

"- and *I* got you someone to wear zebra print undies, you naughty boy," reminding him of my introduction to Meg.

"I've got my career to think about, Nate."

"*I* don't want to think about being lunch," I said.

Jeff took a breath, the kind a friend takes when they're about to tell you something important that you're not going to like, like they just stole your home entertainment system, ...they did your girlfriend, ...or, they did your girlfriend while stealing your home entertainment system - twice. Like an automatic assault rifle, he let it rapidly rip, "You will do it and you will be responsible for him or your psych outburst and treatment will be reported to the state licensing board as not being fit to practice and you'll lose your license." He grew even quieter as Bakuya came out from his hut with what appeared to be his travel belongings, "Try fighting your malpractice trial with *that*."

Now, *I* was hoping Blow Gun Bob would take me out. This nightmare in my mind's eye would have to wait however, as a loud slapping noise returned my senses back to the present moment. Bakuya had struck Dengon's hand as he reached for the leather pouch slung over Bakuya's shoulder in an attempt to properly load the vehicle. Either he was keeping his carry-on, I thought, or perhaps checking to see if a little meat tenderizer was needed to make Dengon's flesh a little more palatable.

ENTRY 6

I couldn't quite figure out the witch doctor. He sat there in the jeep's backseat like a macabre five star general – proud and matter-of-fact, as if ready to command a legion of zombies into a brain eating frenzy. Yet, he said he had never been in such a magic moving box as our four wheeled scrap heap. He didn't act surprised or scared, just like he belonged. The thought was always there in my mind that he could've been focusing on his next meal. I focused a death grip on the wheel following the directions of our GPH or, Global Positioning Human – Dengon, who with his late directions and wild pointing antics, was quite the jerky GPS.

"You sure you want to drive?" asked Dengon when he saw my angry white knuckles tensely curling around the wheel, forward and back.

"Can't do worse than you did," I shot back and then asked, "Does he look hungry to you?" as I scrutinized the cannibal in the rearview mirror.

Jeff stretched comfortably in his seat, "Relax, Nate. He'll have more than enough groceries to eat when we're home."

Mark snickered from the back seat and leaned forward to half whisper, "Just remember to sleep with one eye open and hope he doesn't switch your Old Spice with Open Pit."

I hated it when they punched my buttons and thus declared, "One more word back there and so help me, I'm turning the cannibal around right now."

When we finally got to the airport, I was relieved she was there, the sun glistening off her smooth skin, too hot to touch. I couldn't wait to board her. But the witch doctor just sat there in the jeep staring at her tail. He then turned his head looking at the rest of the rest of her body.

"Never seen a plane before?" Dengon asked. Obviously, he hadn't. Bakuya was either too stupid or too proud to go ahead and tell us that he wanted to go back.

"Tell him it won't crash," Jeff directed to Dengon. "And should it, ask him if he eats his road kill," I added, while Dengon explained that these were the "birds" that made those great billowy white poop streaks across the sky as seen from the ground. I guess that was easier for Dengon than trying to explain the science behind the vapor cloud contrails of a plane's engine to a savage.

Though he cautiously looked it over with a great amount of uncertainty, he boarded.

In the air, each member of our ulteriorly motivated, dysfunctional group soon was fast asleep in his seat. This one drooled, that one snored, while another cuddled a pillow. Even Bakuya was fast asleep in the seat next to me after a while. I, however, only rested with eye closed. Singular - eye. Aye, the other that was closest to the cannibal frequently roved up and down him so as not to become an in-flight snack.

I marveled at how there could be any primitives left in the world with technology the way it is. Even from the missionaries who had encountered them; he'd *have* to know of the better things of the outside world. If not from *them*, then any other outsiders he and his tribe had met. Didn't those things make him want to help his fellow primitives to a better life? Think of the diseases they would not have to fear anymore. Not having to live in unsanitary conditions. But then, one can't expect too much from someone who's amped up about wolverine urine.

SUPPLEMENTAL ENTRY

My apartment isn't that special. With nobody but me, I don't need a lot of room. As Muntabbi stepped from the cab he shook his feathers like a proud peacock. Then he stood silently as he looked up at the 'wall dwellings' as he called the apartment buildings. Turning with mouth agape, he looked at the other tall 'cliff walls of man,' - these junior skyscrapers, and slung his belongings sack over his shoulder. I found it amusing that anyone could look at the gray weathered brick, their relief worn by years of acid rain, and to perhaps behold what their creators once saw and appreciated when they contemporarily gleamed upon their opening, years ago.

But you can't turn your back on a feral physician for even a minute, as while I tipped the cab driver, I thought it strange Muntabbi spoke in his native tongue to two tattooed city gang members, "Oh," he would later translate to me, "What tribe are you from?" he asked the tough looking youths.

"Yo! Check out the freak," said one that had symbols of death inked from his temples to his jaws.

"Yo! Yo! What kinda steeze he gots?" his homie called out.

Bakuya, for the first time, looked out of his element, "I, I do not understand," he sputtered in English. And he didn't.

Any word, any hint of a 'challenge,' could get you a hollow point slug where you least of all needed one. In the ER we deal with rough customers often - *after* they have gone through metal detectors and security. Hospitals should be a safe haven. Free of concern from violence. Warring nations even recognized that a Red Cross insignia on a white background meant that whatever it adorned was a non-target entity – if that nation had any kind of honor. Today, hospitals are like their own little airport TSA zones looking for that potential rogue individual. However, while an extra suitcase gets you an extra fee from the terminal's gate agent, the ER doesn't charge extra for your emotional baggage that you carry on. On these streets, you're naked and exposed, at the mercy of human behavior elements. You hope that any sputtering electrical brain synapses of some stranger you meet doesn't arc to cause a mental short circuit, leading to trigger-finger seizures.

Another of the gang's posse had joined up to scope out the action and grabbed a feather from Bakuya's clothing - if you could call it that - and looked at the non-native, native's bare feet, "You a fly bum? You need some trainers on those naked dogs."

Nervously, I thought about throwing open the cab door and stuffing Bakuya back in, but the cabbie must have sensed trouble and wanted no part of it. For, having gotten his money, with a stomp of the gas pedal, he was gone.

"Show respect," ordered Bakuya, "I am Bakuya Muntabbi, Grand Tribal Healer of the Wammami clan."

Laughter, they say, is the best medicine. My jury is still out on that one, but it definitely offers a nice diversion. I took advantage of their mirth to walk up the curb without making eye contact. The gang members couldn't see much anyway, as their eyes were filled with tears, breathless from laughing so hard. I grabbed the witch doctor as I passed without a pause and yanked him into my building beyond the security door.

"Don't be dissing us fly bum," I heard one of them shout as another added, "Man! Weird-bird."

The gangers studied Bakuya for a moment before they left. Not having a, *Domesticating and Caring for Your Feral Bushman* textbook in my bookcase, this wouldn't be easy, it was going to be mission-friggin'-impossible.

"Look, things are *different* here," I admonished, "If they think you're dissing them, I mean, disrespecting them, they'll kick your booty to Djibouti - or worse."

"Children respect elders," he stated, as if reciting a bylaw, sadly, from Victorian times.

"Oh, witchy, you've got a *lot* to learn," I said as we got into the elevators, "You've jumped out of your jungle and landed in one, more menacing. The civilized world."

"Civilized?" he asked, as if both digesting the meaning and scoffing at the concept. This new reality was now before him ... and me. Oh, how I'd like to kick Jeff's ass.

I unlocked my apartment and ushered the witch doctor in. This drew strange looks of disapproval from my elderly neighbor and snoop, Mr. Finch, who passed by in the hall.

Once inside, I announced, "This is it." I pulled a souvenir brassiere from a previous, more whimsical past evening, off the lampshade to toss behind the couch.

"What was that?" he asked, referring to the disappearing undergarment.

"Double barrel slingshot."

"Double slingshot? I must get one for hunting back home." He perused curiously about the room. He stared at the bright light bulb in the floor lamp, "I've never been this close to such a tiny sun." He looked out the window at the view and then squinted hard at the inactive TV screen next to it, "this window is dirty. You cannot see through it."

I only begrudgingly admit here, privately, that there was a moment of refreshing innocence about the savage that intrigued me. They're so darn cute at the explorative age, aren't they? But then, he had *me* in his sights I began to worry.

"I'm hungry, Gnat."

I grabbed his arm and pulled him into the kitchen, avoiding his eyes, to search for whatever food was available lest I become the 'snack' and said, "*Nate*. For the *millionth* friggin' time." I looked in the fridge and found an old piece of fried chicken. Yeah, fried chicken, that'll work. That keeps well. So what if it's a couple weeks old. It's practically bomb shelter food and perhaps an upset tummy for the WD will keep me from becoming a BM.

"This is what we call a 'drumstick' here. Food," I said, before I tossed it into the microwave and began to heat it. I pulled up my pants leg as far as I could and pointed to the exposed area, "And this is what we call a 'thigh.' Not food."

I wasn't sure I was getting through as Bakuya only rolled his eyes and said, "I do not eat Gnat."

"*Na* --" I began to correct again, "--never mind." I figured that I'd settle and be happy if we could just keep the menu items straight.

The beeping of the microwave startled Bakuya. He was at once entranced by the gently steaming chicken piece as it was pulled from the "magic metal cook box." He looked underneath it, around it and inside of it, wondering where the flame to heat it had come from. He took the chicken leg and bit into it heartily with his ugly notched teeth.

"Mmmmm. Is good," said Bakuya.

"Yeah. Open your mouth," I instructed, then took a look for a brief oral exam. His teeth were honed to points or notched in their middle, part from never knowing fluoride and part what appeared to be ceremonial creations. I told him, "We'll need to get you to a dentist before you go back to the bush. Speaking of which, I still have a good part of it on me."

I really needed to jump into the shower and figured Bakuya couldn't get into too much trouble while he was still working on that drumstick. For extra insurance, I turned on the television - the ultimate bad babysitter. Bakuya was transfixed by the flashing images.

"What is this?" he asked.

"Television. Ultra Hi-def."

"Window view keeps changing, yet doesn't move."

"Enjoy that, I'm washing up," I added as I went into the bathroom.

Maybe my brain had a mild case of jungle rot, because I should've been smarter than to think everything would be fine. Sure it started with innocent touching of the screen frame. It was even rather amusing as he tried to peer inside it, literally, as he gently smashed his nose against the fifty-five inch LED screen. He wasn't knocked out – unfortunately - for he was still able to see a small fly that rested on the top of the TV take wing to explore behind the set. *My* inquisitive little guest likewise stuck his head behind the television, just as a hi-def image of a flower came onto the screen where a large fly - magnified all the more by the camera lens - landed on the petals. That sucker had to be about two inches long on screen. When Bakuya looked again at the front of the TV, he let out a shout at how his little friend had suddenly 'grown.'

Before I even realized what was happening, before I could utter a sound at his alarm, the witch doctor swatted the pixelated pest, sending the one thing that gave me comfort, crashing backwards off its stand. It died in a puff of smoke, its little circuit board soul wafting up to Heaven. I closed my bathroom door in mourning, the sounds of my sobs drowned out by the water streaming from the showerhead.

I was totally oblivious to how hungry he was, for after he had finished the drumstick, he gnawed on its bone before going into the kitchen to open the fridge. He pulled out the package of Kowalski FootLongs and stuck them in the microwave. He apparently loved the sound of the beeps emanating from pushing the various buttons on the microwave control panel almost as much as he loved the meat shrapnel that he scraped from inside the oven after the hotdogs exploded. Fleshy fireworks. It just doesn't get any better than that if you're a cannibal. Except maybe for the knock at the door that I was totally oblivious to in the shower.

The salesman standing there in the doorway had probably never come face to face with an authentic witch doctor before. But this was just another big city with its requisite one-offs and he was a true prattle professional, launching rapid fire into his pitch, "Hi sir, your neighbor let me slip in to talk to him and I wanted to meet the rest of the tenants to tell you about the fantastic opportunity to buy a subscription that will change your life."

Bakuya only stared blankly at the man.

The salesman wouldn't give up, "You live here?"

Bakuya seemed to nod, though perhaps it was just recoil from the frankfurter induced fart. '*But he seemed so friendly,*' Bakuya would later tell me, as he ushered the guy in while I was still blissfully ignorant, toweling off and blow-drying. This salesman jumped on his now hooked sucker, like a long marooned pirate riding a two-bit tart.

"Now," he continued, looking to seal the deal, "I just need to get an address. Oh, how about I just take it off of that junk mailer on the end table there to make it easy?" Upon seeing him reach for his pen, Bakuya knew paper must be involved. He picked up the worst paper he could have from the end table near the door and then forked it over before he went into the kitchen to play with the microwave some more.

"Direct deposit check stub," the salesman mumbled while he studied the name/address, account and Social Security number on it. I was just a few minutes too late as I found Bakuya closing the door shut.

"Where were you going?" I asked him, and then at the crackle of sparks, "Is the microwave still on?" I ran into the kitchen and found an unopened metal can of beans sparking away in the microwave. It shuddered and danced around like an epileptic moth in a bug zapper. Quickly, I grabbed the witch doctor and pulled him down to the kitchen floor before I could utter an obscenity - barely a moment before the *BLAM*! The force blew open the microwave oven door, while a sharp twisted piece of can metal broke through the oven door glass and imbedded itself into its mesh. Apparently, he had found the *incendiary* setting.

Bakuya slowly rose up and I with him, locking my eyes into his. I didn't want to forget for one moment that this was a hapless bushman, because I probably would've killed him right there. The kitchen and everything in it, was covered with the spewed baked beans and chili sauce - including our faces, mildly burned by the napalm-like goo. Taking a finger he wiped a streak of chili from my face, as if creating a war stripe, then sucked on the digit and proudly proclaimed, "Ah, ready!" Now on the face of it - pun or not - he was of course talking about the chili, or perhaps *me* with the chili as a condiment. Although I was more worried his tone seemingly spoke of what lay ahead. You know, like a drill sergeant about to put a recruit through boot camp Hell Week?

ENTRY 7

I don't remember collapsing into bed. I crashed the moment my head hit the pillow. I had dreamed of Africa, of its beasts and animals upon its plains and deserts. Fittingly, my mouth was dry and my tongue had shriveled like a dried chili pepper. Exploding *chili* - it was all a bad dream, I hoped. The sudden pumping of rap music confirmed then that I wasn't alone. I groaned as I dragged my sorry ass from beneath the comfortable covers. "It wasn't a nightmare," I complained like a kid being told there was no 'snow day' break from school after all.

After I stumbled into the living room, I found Bakuya squinting in front of the old, tiny color set that I had dug out of storage and rigged to a digital converter box. The small analog set looking far too retro where the flat screen had previously sat, bathed Bakuya in the toxically mesmerizing cathode ray beams of MTV-like videos. He stared at the rap group, its screen image fuzzy with low-def static. He explored like a two-year-old would, touching the bent coat hangar jammed into the opening where the antenna had broken off, making the picture a little clearer. I smirked as he discovered standing on one foot changed the reception again. Next he moved his free arm this way and that, each time with a resulting change in the quality of the images of the adoring crowd and the performing rappers on the stage. He, at times, made the picture better at the same instant that applause erupted for the on screen performers.

"This clan has respect," Bakuya said in reference to the continued props given to the rap stars. He seemed surprised by the reaction of the audience, as I've always been, because to me, carrying a rhyme isn't the same as giving someone back their time on planet Earth in my humble opinion. Speaking of which…

"Work time, Muntabbi."

Feathers and beaded loincloths really don't go with stethoscopes and white coats. I took him down to the men's clothing store. I wondered how impressed he would be after he stepped into some new threads and further into the twenty-first century. First I had him try on a suit - nothing too flashy - I didn't want to inspire him to further embellish with any bones or feathers.

He emerged from the dressing room. He looked at his arms and legs and rubbed against the itchy wool garment like an early grade-schooler trying on his first suit. Now I know how my mother must have once felt. He looked at himself in the mirror and shook his head vigorously in the negative. I reached over to the rack and pulled off a blazer for him to try on instead. Something a little less formal, but still he wasn't happy.

I took it down a notch to a shirt and tie, same result, not happy.

"What do you want? I got to get to work!" I said.

He thought for moment before a broad smile, similar to a shark's, broke out across his face. A brief time later and we're emerging from the, *Dawg Pound Clothes* hip-hop clothing shop, right next-door to the men's store, the one with the sign that read, "Do it Dawggy Style." - I don't think I need to describe their logo. Bakuya stood there in the only outfit that grabbed his eye - dressed like a rapper's rapper. He switched on his LED Scrolling Belt Buckle that electronically flashed, *Shake it like a Shaman*. Artificial 'bling' hung from his neck and the trinkets, flashing in the sun, dazzled him.

"Rappers are supposed to act cool and *indifferent* to their own coolness," I deadpanned.

"Coolness? I will see if they have ice," he chirped, but I grabbed his arm and hurried him in the direction of the medical center.

Rather than walk through the entire hospital, I decided that going directly through the ER entrance would be the shortest path, not to mention the quickest baptism of fire for the witch doctor. What to me was another day in the "pit" was seen through fresh eyes as a place of wonder. What I've tuned out long ago, either through constant desensitization or self-preservation, he tuned into. He seemed aware of everything all at once, taking in every person and every event around him near the entrance.

Bakuya listened intently as a siren approached, "It's as if demons scream."

"Ambulance siren," I said, "We hear, we come."

I needed to move him further inside and quickly, before he might make me *sense* the environment again, and we don't want *that* to happen. Once inside, of all the things that caught his attention was the wall mounted TV, running a commercial of an elderly, kind, aproned lady who tried to get her husband to eat as if he was a child, telling him, "Open up and let the airplane fly in." He didn't even notice Jeff who paused in passing and whispered, "There you are. Any movement?"

"I tried money, offered to find wolverine urine, even offered to piss like one - no go," I said, "Don't know what else this guy wants, but I want him out." I might as well have been talking to a wolverine's ass, as Jeff only waved over his shoulder as he headed out the door beneath the television. "You owe me a microwave and a hi-def TV," I called after him. Still, I couldn't hate Jeff. Not with the images of blue people, the weak and the dead, necrosing on the TV screen with the caption, "Goliath: **Virus Armageddon** – Tonight at 10." Yeah, ...I guess every time or two life kicks you in the ass to see if you're paying attention.

"Gnat TV deaf and mute," said Bakuya comparing what he watched now to my busted set.

"It is now," I replied in reference to it.

I grabbed a Visitor Pass from the fatigued security guard's desk, "Gotta write your name," I told him. I scribbled, *B.M. Big* and pasted the sticker onto the center of Muntabbi's upper chest.

He studied it and then asked, "It says Grand Tribal Healer of Wammami clan?" as if wondering how so few letters could say so much.

"In English it does," I replied.

Hey, don't think *that* about me reading this, get that thought out of your head. Here's a newsbreak: saints live in heaven, I live in Detroit. I blow off steam just like you - and I'll feel like a prick for doing so afterward.

As I observed him, I imagined the witch doctor walking in the cave of a lion's den. I noted the wariness of his every step, his mouth slightly agape at the noise and sights and smells of the E.R. A nurse hurried a cranky, bloodied patient with bruised face past us. His face was partially covered by bandages limiting his field of vision and he left a nice bloodstain on my sleeve when we accidentally collided. I grabbed him and peeked under the bloody facial dressing, "He'll need a facial bones CT and that shredded lip'll need plastics," I told her.

As she hurried him away, Bakuya posed the following, "Gnat, why do people not bow before their healer in this cave of a million moans?"

"Have *you* got a lot to learn," I answered, and wondered what the first chart of the day would bring.

As we made our way to the first case, I could feel the witch doctor's eyes upon me. Not in a menacing way, but rather one of befuddlement - wanting to help all those poor moaning souls lying on carts in the hallway.

"Now that's what I wish I had," came the old cantankerous voice from one of the carts, to Bakuya. The crusty man explained further upon Bakuya's clueless look, "A big B.M. Like it says on your shirt." The man tugged on Bakuya's shirt a little to emphasize the scrawl I put on his nametag, which Bakuya tried to explain, "It proclaims me to be –"

"- A pooper! That's what I hope they give me. So I can get out of here!

Bakuya saw me stifle a grin, "Well," I said, "those *are* your initials. But what does a tired gnat know?"

An even more tired Dr. Nimbett used what energy he had left after the night shift to make certain our entrance was his eager exit. Nothing better than getting off a twelve hour shift.

"Nate, good to see you. 'Finished what I had, new cases are yours," he said.

If I tossed a pillow on the floor he probably would've dove onto it like gold medal swimmer, Michael Phelps. Sleep deprivation is an assassin. You gain weight, you're moody, and you fall asleep at the wheel on the way home and lose control of your car, crash and die – like a friend of mine, who left behind three kids and a wife who later became an alcoholic.

"Get a good rest," I called after him.

"I'll try not to fall asleep at the wheel and make more work for you. But if my lotto numbers hit, you're working a *double*."

Bakuya hadn't quite understood the exchange, but he was taken aback at the comment. He later told me that he felt that a healer should stay until all those brought before him have been taken care of. Poor savage, he doesn't know in our jungle there is no end to those needing alleviation from pain and suffering.

"Medicine men here are weak, they have cast away their spirit" said Muntabbi.

"Weak?" I asked, "Come here." I led Bakuya to the trauma room to show him our jungle in its entire gory splendor. There, on carts with blood-soaked sheets, lay two youths. They were of an age that everyone laments is much too young to die. No wonder Dr. Nimbett was so tired. "Behind door number one, we have two rival gang bangers who shot each other." We were just in time to see the orderly pull the sheet over the head of one, the endotracheal tube was still protruding from his mouth.

"What is he smoking?" asked Bakuya in reference to the breathing tube. I ignored the question as an orderly answered, "Argument over tennis shoes. So stupid." The orderly didn't grimace, didn't even shake his head, as it's become all too old-school for those who work in the pit. I took Muntabbi to the next room and quickly looked over the nurses' notes, which were left at the bedside.

"Here we have an abandoned elderly lady," I said, "her family threw her out as she was too much to care for." Sometimes, the family never even comes in. There's only the positive tail light sign as the bewildered granny (or grandpa) is dropped off with a suitcase at the entrance, the car pulling out and quickly turning away down the driveway.

It was here that I couldn't believe myself - that I could perhaps actually start to see the witch doctor as somebody who did "treat" people, because there was an almost ethereal element that took over his being, a "compassion" in his eyes. I remember that look, I used to have it when I first began this. Too many endless nights combined with too many unending days of pain, depravity and sorrow force an 'overwrite' of your mental security codes to help you survive it all. As you lose that look, your reflexes become sharper. You watch your front and you watch your back. I watched as a small, white, tiny wiggling form writhed off the edge of the cart. The wormlike shape continued its writhing on the floor and made a soft little crunch as I crushed it with my heel. "Don't mind the vermin," I said. I pulled back the sheets to reveal open bedsores on the bottoms of the poor elderly woman's legs. They were filled with the rest of the crushed maggot's family and friends who decided to stay behind and continue consuming the feast of the foul smelling, rotted flesh. Each wiggled around, seemingly to jockey for position, all the better to gorge its banquet.

I decided to summarize the remaining potpourri of pain: "Rape victim over there, terminal cancer patient over there," as I point toward each of the curtains that afford the exam carts a small measure of faux privacy. A male nurse whisks an ashen colored man down the hallway past us to the cardiac cath lab.

"There goes a man with a broken heart of the worst kind," I explained, "And down there we have our police holding area, where if you're too drunk or too violent and no doctor in his right mind would see you, we will." I wasn't certain how much had registered, as he was lost in the large mural on the wall of the E.R. Peds wing – one of happy smiling cartoon characters. I wondered if his impression of the art mimicked that of my own when I had once first glimpsed it: characters of mirth and fun, their permanent fixed grins mocking the realities that pass before them of ill and injured little bodies and being mocked themselves by it all.

"Those are an illusion, Bakuya. Kids don't come here cause it's a happy place. They're ill. Abused."

"You heal them," he retorted.

"No. I help them. Sometimes. Sometimes not. I ask myself, does it ultimately matter? All the misery, when we're all going to die anyway? The inhumanity. Is our work wasted when life does *it* to us again and again? Worse yet, when we just do it to each other again and again?"

Silence. I guess I had a few poison darts of my own. Then life returned fire, with arrows of lust as Roxie Preminger and her briefcase stopped at the nurses' station. If goddesses wore pinstripes, Zeus would be in *her* lap taking dictation. She wasted her talents as far as I was concerned. She could've been a model instead of the Preminger Pharmaceutical representative, as her nametag read. A tag I read every time, letting my eyes linger over voluptuous curves, longer than they should. But to me and the other doctors she was, "Ah, the free pen person," I said and hurried over.

"Heard about Stabilolol?" Roxie asked me while she held out glossy detail fliers and refrigerator magnets with the drug's logo, "Lowers blood pressure with less than half the side-effects of regular beta blockers."

"Barely," I said to better stay in her presence and take in her sweet scent. Oh the heavenly aroma of her faint perfume – a balm to the smell of stool and assorted other nastiness in the room air, "Here Bakuya, have a magnet."

My attention however was diverted as Bakuya dropped the magnet and it stuck to the metal trim strip on the nurse's station counter. Bakuya had tried to catch it with a hand cupped beneath its presumed path to the floor, but it hung on to his surprise, not giving up its hold to the steel counter strip.

"Oh! Oh!" he softly exclaimed pointing wildly, perhaps imitating the first Homo sapiens to discover magnetism. I ignored him as the drug rep talked on despite some bewilderment at the animated bushman. He slowly pulled the magnet away. He tried to stick it to his forehead. Then to his disappointment, he tried to stick it to my back. He stuck it to the metal rail of a passing patient's cart. He removed it before the gurney continued being pushed on its way by an aide. Then stuck it again to the next passing cart's rail. I was struck by the sense of wonderment that something so simple had caused in this grown man. And then, by the sense of panic I felt when he missed the railing and it landed on the left upper outer chest of a patient who had a pacemaker! The magnet fouled the pacer and the old man became rather woozy there on the cart.

"I'd also mention that Preminger Pharmaceuticals is the only company right now whose work is close to completion on a cure for Goliath," she continued. It was then, when the patient threw up on the floor, that I noticed the offending magnet and quickly yanked it off his chest. He began to feel better very quickly.

"Don't do that," I said, and tossed the magnet onto Bakuya's belt buckle where it instantly went blank.

"They're hoping to test it soon," added Roxie, "Check back with me next month for any progress."

"I'll make a note of that," I said and sensed that my attention on Bakuya was a turn off for her.

Jeff came over and sensing fresh meat, she straightened her pinstriped jacket and skirt, "Hello there, doctor."

"I'm not a doctor," said Jeff, "and I'll add I'm a happily married man." He did not stop but nodded at Bakuya and I, and continued on as Roxie smiled and looked at him out of the corner of her eye.

"I'll make a note of *that*," I said to myself.

"Guess who's back," chided Nurse Sierra, having spotted us down the hall.

Bakuya had given me disapproving looks at my overly warm attention to Roxie. But when he saw

Sierra, there was a spark in his own eyes it seemed. I wondered how Sierra would take to wearing a bridal bone through her nose? Evidently, Bakuya wondered the same thing asking, "Excuse me, pretty lady are you available?" She politely covered her disinterest. When a woman can totally shoot you down yet make it seem like you still made her smile - now *that's* art.

A moan came from a treatment room. I knew that moan. It sounded familiar and faux. There in the treatment room was the injured wrist patient.

"Oh no, not you," the injured wrist patient groaned while he held his flanks. I asked him what brought him in despite seeing his posture.

"Didn't injure it doc," referring to his back, "Disc problem in the lumbar area. Oh, the pain. I can't take it anymore," he groaned as Bakuya's eyes narrowed on the man.

"I've already offered you alternative treatment," I said.

"But I'm really hurting this time."

"Gnat, you must help him." Bakuya joined in.

"Finally someone who cares," the patient said in a performance worthy of an Actor's Guild card. Because while the doctor is a professional when it comes to the practice of medicine, patients purely seeking pain medication are professional in their own right.

"Look," I whispered to Bakuya, "this guy's a fraud. Trust me, okay? He has an addiction to pain killers."

"You called *me* 'fraud,'" said Bakuya unwilling to leave it alone.

The patient's lip quivered at quelling a grin, most likely happy to have an enabler at his side. I told Bakuya, "Never mind," to quell his insistence. I was pissed off at his interference and the fact that he's from a warp zone so far removed from this garbage, where the sick were truly ill and no one was looking for their next fix.

"I'll be happy to give you an ibuprofen if you have pain, but we have nothing else to offer you," I told the patient and left with Sierra to give him a moment to either think about my offer or to walk out. I left Bakuya behind as a parting gift. This was my mistake because he had pulled out a small section of bamboo from his leather bag. It had been hollowed out and corked on both ends. From it, he carefully measured out a white powder mixture into one of the disposable cups and made a gesture with his hand for "his" patient to gulp it down.

While I was busy with discharge instructions at the desk and trying to get the person on the other end of the phone to believe, 'No, I didn't order a subscription to *Clog Monthly* nor, mink pot holders either,' as I was apparently cursed again by the insidious witch doctor and interrupted by Sierra, "You have to come see this," she said.

There in the exam room was the injured wrist and back pain patient sitting motionless with a dreamy, dazed expression.

"Pretty colors. Whoa," he said.

"What did you do?" I demanded.

"I cured him," Bakuya answered.

"You gave him his buzz!"

"You should take a lesson from this guy, doc," oozed the patient, "Hey B.M., you got an office around here?"

"I cured him," Bakuya repeated.

"Are there any loose body parts around the department today?" I asked Sierra.

"Why?"

"Keep a tight count," I said and nodded at the witch doctor, "it's almost lunch."

ENTRY 8

I slouched in the chair at my kitchen table feeling every bit like a crumpled heap. I drifted off for a bit, a bad dream my only entertainment. Truly, I was convinced that there would be no other outcome for me than raving insanity from living with the witch doctor, especially after I awoke and saw him enter in his tribal bonnet, wearing a "BBQ" grilling apron that I had forgotten about. He set a bowl of food down before me with the comment, "Nurse Sierra is most beautiful."

"I don't think she'd be much of a happy hutwife with a bone through her nose."

He only grinned and encouraged me to, "Try it," as he pushed the bowl a little closer to me. I studied the slop that looked like rotted leftovers and imagined that at any minute, a tentacle would rise up from the surface, grab me by the neck and pull me in.

"No thanks," I said.

He persisted, "Open up and let the airplane fly in."

I pursed my lips. Was he kidding?

"Casts out your evil spirits," he added.

"I don't need…"

However that was all Bakuya needed to pinch my nose closed, my mouth already open in protest, now forced wide to heed the call of my lungs for a breath. He crammed a spoonful of the ooze in. It had a barely familiar taste, yet different from any culinary morsel I've ever experienced before.

"Tastes like chicken. What is it?" Then he told me.

"Fresh made. Recipe for old man."

My eyes felt as if they'd left their sockets. I spit out the – whatever part it once was, jumped to my feet, and bolted out of the apartment, ruffling Bakuya's feathers as he looked on after me. I sprinted into the hallway trying to keep from vomiting the human protein I had just been told I consumed. I stopped and pounded on the door of my elderly neighbor.

"Mr. Blainly? Mr. Blainly!" I called.

The door slowly opened and the old man stood in the doorway, "What?" he asked. He *was* there, oh what a sight to behold. Jowls that hung like a Bulldog's face in the middle of July, jowls that were as wrinkled as his white tank top and boxer shorts that he seemed to have momentarily forgotten was all he currently wore. Of course, he looked no more the mess than Mrs. Wieder, the widow from the floor below but every bit as startled, trying to cover her sheer, skimpy nightgown with throw pillows from the couch. The outdated curlers in her hair bounced madly about as she looked for an exit to conceal her dignity, or at least what was left of it. They really should never give Viagra to a man old enough to make dust a respectable shelf accessory.

"Well? What the hell do you want?" he asked.

"Oh, um, nothing, I forgot," I tried to recover. Quickly, I rushed down the hall demanding my brain cells erase what they just saw and pounded my fist on the next door. That unit's occupant wasn't inside, but had arrived from behind me rather curious. "Mr Finch. There you are. Alive and in good health I see." I noticed his bandage dressed fingers supported his grocery bag, "Those fingers aren't missing tips, are they?"

Bakuya sighed while collecting me when he tossed the apron over my head and yanked me gently by the neck with it, "Come along, Gnat."

"Just making sure," I whispered to Bakuya. Making sure, that is, that he didn't use any residents in the recipe. "That yak jerky in your pouch *is* yak jerky, right?" I nervously added.

"It's getting mighty weird around here," Mr. Finch called after us.

But, my little journal friend, it's all good, because evening will come. Later, I adjusted my freshly pressed collar remembering having written this last sentence. It kept me going as I consumed myself with the thought of my date with Candice tonight, musing how the evening plans would go and how I hoped it would end up.

"Where are we going?" asked Bakuya as he watched me put on my tie.

"I'm going out, and when I get back, you're going out. To the lobby."

His digesting what I meant gave me just enough time to add the final throw loop to my necktie. I've never been a necktie guy, that's why I wear scrubs.

"I am supposed to follow you to learn your medicine."

"Not this kind," I said.

"Then you must not want the decoction to help your tribe that badly."

"I couldn't care less one way or the other. It's mainly mass hysteria anyway."

"To ignore one's tribe is to ignore one's self."

"Speaking of which, this self is having some fun now," and with that, I left him there in the apartment to do whatever witch doctors do when they're in for the night.

The whole evening flew by as we caught the late act at the local comedy club. Candy loved to laugh, she was the only person I knew who the more she laughed, the more intoxicated she got – without any alcohol – the wilder she became. She once told me that she conditioned her mind to it. Or maybe it was that her brain conditioned her. It didn't matter; she too, has seen too much pain, aspirated and drowned in too much soul withering sorrow. So much that she said, when she got a 'life transfusion,' anything went.

"Wanna see my candy cane stripe impression?" she asked as we arrived back at my apartment door.

"Is it sweet?" I asked coyly while unlocking the door.

"You tell me," she said, as she grabbed onto my shoulders and hopped up to wrap her legs around my thighs like the stripes that twist around that well known confection and yes, every bit as sweet. The tops of her feet held fast against my legs pulling her pelvis tight against mine. In a furiously passionate lip lock, I fumbled to thrust the key into the lock. I wished a good fob for keyless entry were available for bachelor 'wall dwellings.' I wished for more Candy. Finally I got it in, and the cylinder clicked open as I stumbled into my dark apartment through the door with my hands full. Then it happened, *squaaark, bluuurb.* – don't you hate it when your stomach makes noises just at *that* time.

"I just thought. We never had dinner," I said when I could work a lip corner free.

She peered into my eyes as if hoping to find something. I've seen this look before. The search to find what isn't there. What never was there, yet she still decided, "You know you don't need to bother with that stuff first, don't you?"

Just two prisoners making good their escape from the Stalag of life, we froze in our tracks as the lights came on.

"You didn't tell me you have a wife," said Bakuya.

Candy released her grip and scampered off into the bedroom leaving me to fume at the intrusive, bead and feather bonneted, wet blanket.

"The pigeons roost on the roof," I said pointing at the ceiling, "your bonnet could use some new feathers." A lacy thong, landed onto my still pointing, erect index finger having sling-shotted out from the bedroom doorway.

"Waiting," came the soft playful voice that was sweeter then a songbird in spring. The only thing that stood between passionate pleasure and me was wearing a smelly bone necklace while going parental on me.

"This is not what you seek," Bakuya told me.

"Look, get lost, I need this."

His wise and knowing posture didn't concern me and with that, I maneuvered around him like a politician taking a question from a taxpayer. Once in the bedroom, I slid the bolt lock into its position on the door frame. Secure in the knowledge that Candy and I were alone, clumsily, I unbuttoned my shirt for but a moment before deciding that buttons took too long. I ripped the shirt open the rest of the way at the sight of Candy's vivacious eyes peeking from over the top of the covers as she giggled.

"I got cold waiting," she said hoisting the blanket more to show me her beautiful naked form that could only have been sculpted by angels. I was so excited, I jumped into bed pants and all, unable to wait any longer.

Candy began to scream. I didn't care what animalistic cries that savage might hear. She screamed again. Not the screams of love's frenzy but rather, of terror. She said the bolt lock knob gently, slowly, lifted by itself and slid open. Confused, I turned to see my roomy in full witch doctor battle gear with rattle and talismans in hand.

"I couldn't have not locked that door," I murmured, while Muntabbi pranced around chanting and shaking his rattle. "What are you doing?!" I pleaded to the shimmying shaman.

He barely paused long enough to say, "It is known by our culture that unless sacred mating ceremony is performed first, evil spirits will follow."

"We've got the raincoat thing covered, thanks," I growled.

Candy however, had already pulled the sheets around her tightly, having hopped up and out of bed to retrieve her clothes off the floor, "I may be a little kinky, but this is beyond my limit," she said before the bathroom door slammed on my plans.

He tried to hide it, but I saw the witch doctor fight to keep from smiling. Bastard.

"Do you know what you've done?" I demanded.

"Bakuya try to help Gnat have firm relationship," he answered.

"I don't *want* a firm relationship, I wanted – never mind. Listen, you gotta understand that it's an eat-drink-and-be-miserable-for-tomorrow-we-may-die life here." Speaking of which, Nurse Candy had just done up her last button as she hurried from the bathroom and out the door, before I could "enlighten" Bakuya.

"Candy!" I called, but it was too late. "Please," I told Bakuya, "I'll do anything to get you out of my apartment. Out of my life."

"I have yet to see what I have come for," he replied.

I hurried out after the girl and heard Bakuya say something that sounded like, "…As it is with you."

ENTRY 9

Some days you look forward to. Some days you dread. Some you just get through. Others are like a homeless thug who snatches your wallet as you offer a buck, then hands you the bill for the cost of the round he just fired into your gut. That's what it's like when you sit down with the attorney assigned to you for your lawsuit. This one, Mr. Gavin Preston, sat across from me at the otherwise empty boardroom table and intensely reviewed his briefs of my case - not that he hadn't probably reviewed them several times before our meeting - but hey, it adds to the billable hours. He wrinkled his face and puckered his lips. It wasn't going to be good.

"The insurance company won't settle for the size of the amount the plaintiff wants," he stated.

That meant we'd be fighting it. It also means a long, slow slog through hell consuming most of your waking moments. "I won't do it. I'm not going to court like a criminal," I answered.

"The choice isn't yours."

He was right. Physicians have only some small input to whether or not to proceed to trial; ultimately the decision is the insurance company's. Lawyers love to tell the physician, *'Nothing personal, just the cost of doing business.* Remember the homeless thug I just mentioned? Same guy.

In my disgust, I made my copy of the chart go airborne into the wall only inches from Bakuya, but he sat unflinchingly in the corner.

"Does he really have to be here?" asked Preston.

"My other curse," I answered, "He doesn't understand any of this anyway. But back to business, I'm *sure* the patient was able to move freely after the paralytic wore off."

Bakuya then opened his mouth proving me wrong again, "Why do people disgrace a medicine man who wants to help others when ultimately, it is great spirits who choose to heal or not?"

Preston smirked at this naiveté while he packed up his briefcase, "Study your deposition. Get plenty of rest. This isn't a sprint, it's a marathon." He gave another disbelieving look at the witch doctor who had gone into a trance-like state, and added, "Leave *him* at home. And for what it's worth? I think you're a good doc."

"Thanks, but you're well paid to say that," I shot back. I followed him into the hallway to add, "You tell the plaintiff and insurance company to stop playing games with my life."

Back in the boardroom, Bakuya chanted and conjured strange gestures with his hands turned up and outstretched before him - like I need *this,* too.

"I'm a human being. I didn't do anything wrong," I shouted out the doorway to Preston who had already turned the corner down the hall.

I shook Bakuya out of his trance and we headed for the cafeteria. There, I had upon my tray, the Heart Attack Special: Two greasy bacon cheeseburgers – double bacon – fries and a double-chocolate cake wedge. As I moved my tray along the food line tray-rails, I noticed that Muntabbi had a sore on the inner aspect of each of his lower arms while he pushed his tray along the rails. A cafeteria worker took notice at the same time and admonished, "You need to get those covered before going to the self-serve salad bar."

"What are those from?" I asked examining his arms.

"These sores were manifest on your spirit," he said.

They were like ugly scabs, but not scabs. They had a depressed center like an ulcer crater, but not an ulceration, and almost bruise-like around the edges.

"I've never seen a lesion like this," I said.

"I saw them. On your soul," he whispered.

He didn't need to whisper, I already knew him to be crazy, and nevertheless I took him back to the E.R. and treated him.

"Did you self inflict these with something?" I interrogated while applying antibiotic ointment and dressings.

"Yes, I did."

All sorts of hideous non-sterile implements began to dance through my mind in a second guess of his answer. It's the doctor in me. I definitely was not prepared for his answer: "As a healer, I took them from your soul. Even now, you are more relaxed."

"Took my mind off things is all," I wearily muttered.

The witch doctor only smiled, obviously sticking to his belief then asked, "Tonight we'll see Sierra?"

"Jeff and Kels."

Those two had called for a meeting and I'd rather sit home and clean smelly sock lint from between my toes than go, but they weren't asking - it was a command. I took Bakuya with me as I figured my apartment would be safer that way. His eyes were wide with amazement as we pulled into the circular drive before the opulent home.

"Does a god live here?" he asked.

"Only in *their* mind maybe," I retorted.

I instructed Muntabbi to wait in the car and had no sooner reached the porch then I smelled something and turned to see smoke pouring out of my windows from his attempt to bring good luck into my car. I hoped that was legal incense he was burning – don't want to have to hire another attorney. I knew then I'd have to take him in with me to the meeting. On the other hand, this could even-the-score with those boogers inside who caused all this mess for me.

Upon reaching the top of the porch, the door wasn't answered by either of the men but rather, "Sierra!" Bakuya hailed adding, "I'm seeing Sierra, Nat."

She could tell that I too, was surprised and offered, "I just got here. Mr. Mitchall's wife asked if I'd get the door while she gets dinner out." I had no clue as to why she should be there but I suspected that Bakuya had a hand in the amalgam.

"You are most beauteous tonight, eh Nat?"

At this remark, she blushed - Nature's makeup – and the way she wore it would put anything at the Neiman Marcus cosmetic counter to shame. She turned on her heel, her little dress beckoning us to follow as its pleats danced around her feminine form.

"Don't embarrass her," I said.

"Nat cares for Sierra?"

"Don't embarrass *us*. These are the hospital heads. Big chiefs. Speaking of which – any chance you collect heads, too? Don't give me that look, a guy can dream."

The patio deck we walked onto looked out over a stunning, beautifully landscaped courtyard. Jeff was sitting there as Meg waved away a pesky wasp and complained how allergic she was to stings. They were sharing a Bloody Mary when Kels greeted us dressed in his golf shirt, the one with its snobbish Country Club insignia on the breast pocket, "...And you must be, Sierra," Kels beamed, "Thanks for coming. Grand Tribal Doctor Muntabbi asked specifically for you to attend."

Doctor!? Really? I couldn't freaking believe it.

Like I couldn't freaking believe how Meg still looked, "Every time I see you Meg, I'm reminded just how much this guy owes me," I said with a gentle elbow to Jeff.

"You had your way," she said, to reinforce the point that their pairing was my free will doing, and yet, a raised eyebrow she privately flashed me seemed as if to refer back to that 'shower' moment.

"Nope. Never quite could. But Jeff got you everything you wanted, home, pets, commitment –"

Jeff reflectively stirred the ice in his drink and added, "- With mortgage and credit debt bundled in the package. I'm waiting for the day you forget to remind me."

Dammit! I paid too much attention to what *was*, instead of what is. Human nature got the best of me - playing out how things might've played out if only they did. Yeah, I don't understand it either but we all do it. It was just that quick moment that Bakuya had slipped from my radar. He caught sight of the little yellow and black striped body of a yellow jacket land on Meg's flower in her sun visor while we had been talking. The witch doctor pulled a small blowpipe from behind his belt and reached into his bag as the insect crawled over into her hair. Maybe due to a tilt of her head, or perhaps a lock of hair stirred by the breeze, the bug raised its posterior to embed the stinger into her scalp.

I couldn't react fast enough. PWOOF! The tiny poison dart flew from the mini-blowgun and impaled the yellow jacket clean though center body and continued along its trajectory, embedding itself with bug, into a ficus tree's trunk. Everyone else was totally oblivious to what had transpired.

"I'm just happy to see you two happy," I managed to say while waiting for my palpitations to cease-and-desist from what I had just witnessed.

"I never miss, Nat," Bakuya said modestly, noting my horror at his demonstrated marksmanship.

Sierra handed each of us a frosted glass with brightly colored liquids that layered out in the glass. A little paper umbrella was poking up out of each. She said, "I understand when we're stressed out *on* the clock. But I refuse to be, *off* of it."

"A *medicinal* remedy?" I asked at the tonic offered, "You're not *off* the clock then, nurse."

"Professional courtesy," she answered.

Bakuya observed us like a professional poker player with a junk hand while Mrs. Mitchall entered the room and called, "Dinner --." The tiny dinner chime in her hand was too much. It made the most annoying ping with the little wooden hammer as she gently struck it, calling the guests to dinner. At least if she had a gong or something – heck, I would've pretended it was playing the final crash note to the rock song, that begs "mama mia" to let me go.

"—With food and drink and deserts provided courtesy of Perminger. Sorry I'm late," Roxie said slightly winded and slightly wrinkled.

Out on the deck the leaves of that ficus tree drooped lifelessly. The dishes from our gastronomic orgy sat on the table with barely a crumb. It was a real feast, with artificial conversation added, but at least it didn't stain my journal pages like the leftover butter biscuit did. Yes, the conversation was so fake, my belief that we have indeed lost the art of talking to one another, was certainly reinforced. Oh, we shout and scream at one another, but the real pitch-and-catch of well thought ideas and feelings is endangered like the coelacanth fish. *No heed except for our own need* - the witch doctor told me that, once. For if we extinguish the voice of a different idea, we are only dousing the flames of the forge that helps refine our own thoughts.

I certainly hoped that whatever we needed to get from the witch doctor would be gained soon. How much can be learned from a man raised in one of the few wilds that remain? Personally, I hoped 'enough' to get my life back.

At the door the guests said their goodbyes. I couldn't believe Meg when she told Sierra, "If I didn't know better, I'd bet Bakuya is interested in you."

"I never wager on anyone for personal gain. It's bad luck," retorted Sierra.

I watched Kels pull Jeff aside into the study while his wife chatted up the departing guests. Before they shut the door, I saw Turffle lean back in a recliner smoking a cigarette. Roxie smiled casually at me, as if stepping around a pedestrian to make the elevator as the last person before the doors closed. Jeff acknowledged her with a short little exhalation before shutting the door the in her face.

I must say Roxie carried herself well at almost getting a door to the nose. It seemed the classic "credit declined" posture - the one where the plastic you're handed back is overdrawn and you're mad as hell but keep an air of dignity. Something loomed in that room, though. Something I wanted to learn.

"Darned if I didn't just break a shoelace," I said to nobody while pretending to retie it, but rather tightened it up to snap it off just where I wanted. I sat on the floor with my back against the wall to better pull my shoe off, as well as the ruse I created. The smell of cigarette smoke mingled with the faint voices that came from under the door and the doorjamb.

"So?" asked Kels.

"Nate's working on it, …slow but sure," Jeff said.

"Slow but sure, is not the *sure and now* that is expected," Dr. Turffle remarked in a toying fashion.

"Nate's just having a tough time," Jeff added.

"Preminger pharmaceuticals is rushing to get a potential cure to market. Millions spent. Still doesn't work right." Turffle huffed.

Kels seemed genuinely surprised when he asked, "I thought Prism was ready to launch theirs?"

"Geez Kels," interrupted Turffle, "I was wondering what the hell you were doing inviting her here."

I didn't understand this last exchange – and was the "her" Sierra? Roxie? Fighting to re-lace my intentionally broken shoestring, the words that were exchanged next were lost to me when Sierra came over and picked up the personalized *Preminger Pharmaceuticals* name pin that had fallen from Roxie's pocket. She read the name aloud and exclaimed, "Roxie? Are you *socialite* Roxie Preminger?"

Roxie hurried over, grabbed the tag and quickly zipped it in her purse as if caught with something obscene while she explained, "Daddy wanted me to learn the company from the bottom up."

Kels had apparently paced just close enough to the door where I could make out: "She came to our office offering to sponsor events. "She paid for --"

"-- We have to get this first. Not Preminger," spouted Turffle.

"I want to see some action, Jeff," said Kels, apparently re-directing the focus, "The hospital and university demand it."

Then those legs appeared next to me. Meg stood there looking over me. I didn't wait for confirmation that she knew I was eavesdropping on the conversation in the other room. My hands exaggerated the knotting of my newly shortened shoelace and I stood up. She didn't say a word. She didn't have to. There was something else on her mind. Something she wanted to know. Something she wanted me to communicate to her. Whatever it was, I had too many questions myself to provide any answers.

In engaging in boudoir maneuvers yet avoiding the abiding bond, I've learned that there *is* this communication wave 'frequency.' Women often do know what they want or sometimes at least what they *think* they want – and saying this could get me thrown out of the International Dude Alliance – but guys simply fail to dial in to that frequency. Sometimes though, there's static on the line, like at that moment. I didn't have time to tune through the interference as Bakuya was about to walk outside with Sierra, but I saw Meg out of the corner of my eye, placing her ear nervously and with uncertainty outside the study door.

I jumped off the porch to the walkway hoping to keep up with Bakuya before he might put Sierra into an embarrassing verbal situation, but he only helped her into her car. She called out as she drove off with a wink, "See you in the pit."

I told Bakuya as he watched her go, "Too bad she's not the type to go down easy," and wasn't prepared for his reply of, "Worse for you, …you *are*." I just looked at him rather dumbfounded. Funny, I never used that word for myself before, but when I came back to Earth, Bakuya was sitting in the car and Roxie walked over.

"Dr. Briggs, I'd love to talk to your friend about jungle remedies some time," she said.

"I'm sure he'd find you quite luscious," I deadpanned softly while looking at him sitting regally in the car.

"Most men do," she said with a flip of her hair and moved with a feigned shyness just a very tiny bit closer to me.

"Well especially Bakuya. Cannibal, you know."

I wondered whether it was that information or my postural rebuff that made her step back in disgust, "Make no mistake, Dr. Briggs, Preminger is interested in alternative therapies. Very interested."

I got in the car next to Bakuya and drove off in time to see her take a perturbed swipe at the shrubbery in my rear view mirror. She nervously looked over her shoulder at me. Bakuya said he too witnessed the same in the passenger door mirror, as well as Dengon emerge from the bush. I quickly looked back again, but there was only Roxie getting into her car.

ENTRY 10

The next day, I had decided to take the good witchy into the O.R. From behind the glass window of the scrub prep room, he looked with fascination at the surgical team and the array of their instruments. They surrounded the draped hump on the table that was the patient who was undergoing a coronary artery bypass operation.

Bakuya stared out at the scene as Sierra stretched a surgical mask over his face and a hair bonnet on his head. Actually it was several bonnets taped together to fit over his headpiece that he insisted he wear to the "healing." She fussed with the zipper on his white coverall suit that fit over his witch doctor garb making him look like a mad housepainter.

"…So, Kels wants him to get a broad overview," I explained to the cardiovascular surgeon, who was somewhat perturbed that his sanctum had been intruded upon. Not just by the witch doctor, but even a common E.R. doc.

"Keep his rattles out of the sterile field," mumbled the surgeon.

Bakuya was ushered in from the prep room by Sierra to the spot where he could watch, "There you go, all zipped," she said checking his suit.

"I am very much looking forward to this sacred magic," said Bakuya.

"Stand behind the doctor, observe, but don't get too close," instructed Sierra.

"Like you and Nat?" he asked. At this, there was a silence so still from Sierra, that it became its own sound. "Back in my homeland, we cover our faces with masks too, but the eyes betray the soul," he added.

She spun him to face the ongoing procedure. He leaned over a little too far and crashed into an instrument tray stand loaded with clamps, hemostats and other assorted surgical tools. The deafening sound of so much metal hitting the floor could've even woke the patient from his drug-induced sleep.

"Nurse, a new set and a walker for the klutz," deadpanned the cardiovascular surgeon.

"His name is Bakuya," I corrected. I felt somewhat like an unappreciated parent, since witchy couldn't or wouldn't call *me* by my correct name. Yet, there I was supporting him. He who came up and stood behind the surgeons, peering over their shoulders into the open chest cavity. He reminded me of the way I cautiously checked the view over cliff's edge back in the Congo.

"Okay, you probably haven't seen this unless you've gutted a wildebeest," lectured the surgeon, "but what we're doing is putting the patient on bypass.

Now." And with that, the cardiac monitor above the head of the anesthesiologist went flat line. The perfusionist checked the machine that circulated the patient's detoured sanguineous fluids through the clear plastic tubing. The bypass perfusion machine oxygenates the blood and flows it onward, back into the patient.

Bakuya peeked around the surgical table drape to see the patient's face. One might think it a rather serene expression if not for the eyelids taped shut with paper tape and a plastic tube protruding from the mouth. "His heart no longer beats," he finally said.

"We're going to work to fix it," answered the surgeon somewhat bored.

"But the spirit will travel from the body," Bakuya said.

"I hope it has its passport to get past the TSA on return," chuckled the surgeon, "I'm soooo good."

"Only at surgery," I groaned, but the team only ignored witchy and I, focusing on their task.

"Confused, it may seek another," Bakuya stressed. Their backs never swiveled but I noticed his breathing increase – Bakuya's, not the surgeon's. The sight of the surgery was perhaps a little too much for Bakuya I thought. I looked into his eyes in an attempt to draw his focus away from the cutting and stitching of the bypass graft before he could pass out and there'd be feathers all over the floor. His eyes had another look, a sensing, and a tracking. I looked closer to get his attention. He turned slowly but gazed as if looking at another standing next to us. There, reflected in his eyes, the open-heart patient who was on the table now was standing next to him. The reflection was as if the patient was looking with us into his own chest, right next to us.

Bakuya twitched and in that moment the light acted as if the reflection in Bakuya's eye reached out with a ghostly hand that was no more than a wisp of bent reflected light. The appendage seemingly disappeared into Bakuya's chest as he fearfully watched it and then screamed! Not a yell, not a war cry, but something guttural and unearthly.

The room snapped its attention, the little "pumper" or bleeding arteriolar vessel, momentarily forgotten. The surgeon broke the one second of silence by unleashing several obscene words followed by, "Get that nut-burger out of my O.R.!"

Sierra stepped forward to try to intervene but Bakuya's eyes were wide with terror, and in a panic he bolted from the room. I followed him into the hallway, only a step behind. Mind you, no more than a step behind, and yet he was gone. Only his discarded coverall suit was there to stumble over on the floor.

"Where'd he go?" Sierra asked.

"Out of my life, apparently" I said. There was no sound of footsteps. Nobody else was reacting as if they had seen anyone running past. I had the feeling that if the witch doctor left without so much as a bouncing broken bead, that he would not be found.

"Damn," Sierra said, as the circulating nurse walked into the hall from the O.R.

"Don't feel too bad for that witch doctor. Just overwhelmed is all," the circulator said to Sierra. She was from a Caribbean nursing program and once told me about how her great aunt practiced voodoo in the islands. I figured she had an understanding of his shock at the open heart.

Their soft continuing conversation faded from my ears as I walked away, then the O.R. nurse said, "Nate? You after him?"

"No. Not now," responded Sierra.

Which was a very odd thing to presume to answer for me I thought, unless this is what was said; "Nate? You're after him?"

ENTRY 11

I lay alone on my living room floor as I figured things and fingered things - like Becky's number as I thought of her. She was a casualty in the campaign for love. Works on the Labor & Delivery floor helping bring life into the world. Her then husband, had - as she told it – beat that life half out of her emotionally, with the other half flogged out mentally and physically. One day in a packed elevator, her mind packed with reflections, her misty eyes filled with emptiness, she dropped the papers she had held. They were divorce papers. I quickly picked them up when a few people left for their 'floor' and handed them back before more people got on pushing us closer. She looked at me with tear sparkled eyes for seemingly having provided that little kindness.

Sad how we live in a world so starved for a bit of benevolence that something so simple may have such an impact. Yet, the conundrum of such starvation is perhaps precisely what makes such an act a social delicacy, savored in the course of our human events. Though she knew my reputation, I felt her breast press closer against my arm than what the crowding passengers would have caused. That little random act of kindness sparked a hope in her eye causing her to want more. Wanting to know what it was like to feel loved. For in her years of marriage, there was only fear. At the appropriately arranged time I walked through the utility room door. She hoped up onto the long discarded exam table and confidently striding toward her, I took her. There in my arms I hugged her. She trembled and I kissed her, gently at first as if asking a permission that seemed never before inquired of her, then hard when affirmed. But I did not *take* her. Not then. For it wouldn't have been for passion, or whatever healing such a moment sometimes brings. I could tell by her eyes, it was confusion. If anything were to happen then, I would be no better then her ex – uncertainty and exploitation all coming at her, leaving her even more questions. Despite what I am, I am better than that.

But as I lay on the living room floor, I replayed the message she left – she was clearly ready, and asked if we could pull an "all-nighter" together. As I was about to dial her number, I pictured it: two shipwrecks naked, holding fast to one another to salvage whatever feeling of life might remain in our bankrupt souls, looted by life's piratical acts. I had dialed her number several times without completing it. My mind was instead being interrupted with a busy signal. Like some brain cell 'call waiting,' this, 'thought waiting,' of just where Bakuya was, garbled all else.

I could almost vividly picture him, there in some nameless Detroit alley, running through the trash littered shadows... Running as he pulled hard on each breath, as he took in his foreign surroundings...

He spied an old forgotten and stripped pay phone on the wall of a long abandoned and gutted gas station. He picked up the receiver, "Hello. Hello. Nat!" But the line to the handset had been cut in a senseless act of vandalism long ago.

"Yo! Hey, heyyy!" came a woman's voice. Bakuya turned to see a young woman in a tight halter-top and high heels wave at a yellow car. The taxicab stopped curbside and she bent forward to shout through the passenger window, the cheeks of her buttocks peeking out from beneath her ultra tight and ultra short shorts, "Take me to this address on Woodward," she said tossing the paper at the cabby. Then she hopped in and they disappeared into the night.

Another cab cruised by. "Yo! Hey... Hey," Bakuya called out hesitatingly. To the witch doctor, this seemed like a magic machine, appearing when needed and to do one's bidding. He hopped in, just as he had observed the woman do.

"Where ya goin'?" the cabby asked.

"Where Nat lives," he answered.

"Where's that?"

"Nat's house."

The driver got out and smartly marched around to the cab's back door. He opened it and grabbed Muntabbi by his shoulders then pulled him from his taxi. In a loud two-and-a-half-packs-a-day gravel voice, he said, "I don't need no whack-jobs in my cab!" and flung the witch doctor onto the concrete pavement. The taxi made a U-turn through a mud puddle that splashed all over Muntabbi.   Oh, what he thought about "civilization" now.

...And that return call to Becky?   It was never made.

Morning seemed to come forever. I called in a marker and got the rest of my shift covered in the E.R. to leave work early.   I couldn't concentrate and administration didn't help any - they got word from the cardiovascular surgeon about what went down.   I learned that I was now forced to find the shaman or, find my body without my head - suitably shrunken, after they detached it of course. Feeling already cursed, I decided I'd request it bequeathed to that surgeon for a Christmas memento - scratch that, the bastard would probably relish such a trophy.

"So you're going to find him?" Sierra asked me, seeing me by my car in the hospital lot.

"Not my choice. But neither is Tuesday," I said in reference to my court crap.

"About that..." she said, and motioned upward behind her back.

I looked up and there in each window across the fourth floor, stood an employee. Each of our co-workers held up a letter before them that spelled out, "G-U-I-L-T-Y."

"We know you did your best," she added, "and that's how the staff feels." My wry grin erased Sierra's. "Hope they don't have jury duty," I said.

She spun around in time to see three tardy employees rush up to the window glass to stand ahead of the others and quickly hold up their letters, "N-O-T." Her cell phone rang and on the speakerphone was the "O" card letter bearer, who juggled the phone and her letter at the same time from up behind the window, "Sorry Sierra, we got held up." Sierra put away her phone, I put away my hope, and then I pulled out of the lot.

ENTRY 12

The witch doctor stacked the dumpster-scavenged old wooden crates at the alley entrance. Taking up a crudely fashioned, primitive hatchet, he lined up his swing on some sad, tiny saplings that had the misfortune of growing between worn and broken city concrete. Yet, they somehow managed to sprout some pitiful foliage that could've amounted to so much more if they had only had the proper chance. He held his strike. Instead, he smiled at the huge redwood tree trunk that caught his eye nearby. A Sequoia? In Detroit?

He walked over to it intending to cleave off a hunk. *Clang* went the hand ax's strike.

"Aay!" called out a wino, "That's a cell tower," - words that didn't register with Bakuya. "Disguised. To class up the city," the wino added, then savored a hit of his muscatel bottle and surveyed the dump-like conditions around him. "It's a start."

Sirens echoed from the distance and the witch doctor practically trembled with joy and dropped his ax.

Walking into the State Bar pub, I looked over the patrons who drank and mingled over the antique wooden bar and neoclassical fixtures. As I scrutinized the crowd, I couldn't help but realize the cliché of a, "million stories in the naked city," no longer applies. They've all been reduced to a tweet, a sound bite, and the occasional 160-character text message. Just like we have. "Witch doctor?" I called out, "Is there a witch doctor in the house?" and summarily was ignored. I hadn't even had one drink.

Speaking of houses, I wish I would've known at that very moment Dengon and a sleazy accomplice were burglarizing my house. Great, huh?

I started out to find Bakuya, but I was at the bar to unwind. I downed a beer and drank in the barmaid, who became likewise interested during our brief verbal exchange by the pitch of her voice when she said, "Oh, you're a doctor?" Those four words fell from her mouth like four reels of a casino slot lining up *Jackpot* straight across. The little flame of interest had been stoked like the flames of the burning building on the widescreen wall TV above the barmaid's head, but I paid more attention to her than the screen.

I shouldn't have. For the timeworn, four-story brick structure was fully engulfed. The blaze itself behaved as if some living evil, gorging upon yet another structure in Detroit that went up for some reason, or none at all. Even after years of dying embers, the old girl never ran out of buildings, the testament of sheer grit of the strength still within her. Even Chicago once burned to the ground, Detroit never has.

Bakuya arrived in a sprint and found the fire trucks converging. He grabbed an old wooden sandwich board sign and chucked it through the abandoned building's windowpane to stoke the fire.

Spotted by the fire fighters, one asked their chief, "What the hell is he doing?" Before an answer could be summoned, Muntabbi scaled the corner side of the vertical building. He used only a gutter downspout and the occasional window ledge for a foothold. Like a mountain goat on 'speed,' he dodged the flames that licked at him from the broken out windows of each successive floor. The fire chief shouted for an inch and half line to be carried up the stairs and instructed police to keep the TV news van's crew back a safe distance.

Muntabbi paused on the corner ledge of the roof. Smoke thick as midnight curled up over its edges as the flames below reached out from whatever openings they could from deep within the structure. He scanned the horizon, searching...

I casually looked up at the wide flatscreen again while the barmaid wrote her phone number on a scrap of cocktail napkin. I now saw the news chopper's live video feed of the man in African native tribal dress. He stood unflinchingly on the edge like a lion surveying his savanna from the cliff. First time in forever that I felt a little at ease at the sight of him – even a bit at peace. I stuffed the napkin into my pocket and excused myself to go chase the witch doctor.

A plastered patron squinted at the screen as I hurried past him while he said, "Ya shore tha's a wish doctor? Looks more like a naked guy with a pheasant ass on his head."

"Call me. Soon," the barmaid said, while she leaned forward to suggestively rest her ample bosoms upon the bar's reflective countertop. I fought my desire to run back to her at the parting gesture she made with her lips, and now, not being able to go out in public at the moment, I grabbed an iced drink from a passing waitress's tray and poured it down inside the front of my pants.

"Chaser," I sheepishly added. Yeah, it's been that long, okay?

Back at the bonfire of the insanities, firefighters in respirators and rescue gear burst out onto the roof from the stairwell door, plumes of thick smoke exited with them as well.

"Nat?" asked Bakuya.

"Easy. We're here to rescue you," wheezed the firefighter through his air mask as more sirens approached.

Bakuya listened as he had before to the noise, only all the more intently and said, "Where is Nat? The demon's siren screams. He hear, he comes."

They charged Bakuya and got tangled up in themselves as he easily escaped them by twisting like a striking cobra and leaping like a gazelle.

Still can't believe what I lost in the shakedown of my apartment that was going on unbeknownst to me at the same time. Pillows ripped apart and things broken that were apparently in their way. Dengon had said he had admired the witch doctor's large, animal bone and tooth necklace and was going to pocket it, but he was interrupted with "We didn't come for dinner bones," his accomplice snapped and so tossed it onto the rest of my belongings they already had shattered.

When I arrived at the news scene, the embers inside still smoldered despite the torrents of water the firefighters continued to pour on the charred interior of the brick building. "Do you have the roof guy?" I asked, referring to what I had observed on the bar's television. But they ignored me. The firm hand of one of Detroit's finest pulled me back from the scene by my shoulder despite my protests.

"I'm a doctor. *You* there!" I shouted to get the fire chief's attention, "Did you capture the witch doctor on the roof?"

"Jumped to the building next door and ran," he said while he spat out soot speckled gray phlegm, then grabbed the sides of his nose with his thumb and index finger to blow the same crap from his nostrils into the street. "My men almost got trapped up there," he continued, "Damn *mountain goat* is what he is."

I looked up at the tall building wondering just how any man could make the canyon-like leap that stretched from the one roof to its neighbor, and live.

Bakuya however had escaped to Shakedown Street. That's what it's called, not even close to its real name. I don't know if any of the locals could recall the actual name without looking at the corner street sign, if, that is, it hadn't been knocked down or stolen for scrap metal.

Bakuya peered around looking very out of place. He hadn't learned the savvy to make an attempt to conceal his clueless 'tourist' status. Although on this street of cheats, frauds, players and cons, a stranger's freakishness was generally ignored. However, it *would* make you a 'mark,' because a Jackson was a Jackson and legal tender for all debts, if you happened to have one on your person.

Marked he was, when he passed in front of a rundown old duplex converted into the *Sojourn of Fortune* tarot card shop. A paroled convict (and still a con man) hailed him from the corner alley and approached like a pastor bringing the good news to his sheep.

"Friend. Friend!" he called to Bakuya as he advanced while he studied him, "You have a sore on your arm? *I* can *heal* it for you for my customary one hundred dollars."

"I don't have one hundred dollars."

"Sympathetic healer that I am, I will do it then for your belt buckle instead."

Bakuya waited to hear more but the con had already sliced off the bandage from Bakuya's arm.

"You are doctor?" asked Bakuay.

"Better, I'm a psychic healer. Power of the focused mind," he answered tapping his temple with the tip of his pointer finger.

Bakuya was bewildered, yet intrigued. He allowed himself to be sat down on the bottom step of the duplex and listened as the con began his bafflegab and put on a pair of latex surgical gloves. He reacted suspiciously to the con and this wasn't unnoticed by the fraudster.

"Gotta take precautions, ya know?" he explained to the witch doctor regarding the gloves, "Now then…" The con began to work his hands around the area just outside of the sore on Bakuya's arm and the con's body began to contort in an opposite direction. Soon he was over the wound area and seemingly from the skin, he produced what looked like raw chicken fat that seemed to wriggle and bleed as he grunted and groaned through his incantations and bogus exertion. If points were given, he did manage to break a bead of perspiration before dropping back against the step and said, "There. There you go. By tomorrow I guarantee it will be gone."

The witch doctor examined the wound like a surgeon who checks the work of his junior resident, never quite certain it's up to par. Furthermore, he was unfazed by the outstretched hand awaiting payment of his flashy buckle.

Bakuya wasn't the only one who took note of the ritual healing. Gypsy Saladin, the tarot shop owner had come out to better study what was going on outside his shop. Bakuya looked at the con as he got back to his feet and told him, "You have a mark on the back of your neck."

"Saw me from down the street did ya?" replied the con, knowing that the large hairy congenital birthmark was readily visible, and wondered if perhaps Bakuya was more of a rival who had come to Shakedown Street to run his own game and squeeze his corner of the turf. But the witch doctor only replied in a calm, soothingly innocent voice, "I will heal it now for you and we will be even."

"Oh, right," replied the con playing along, "Well, yeah, but I'm owed the buckle if you fail."

"Agreed."

Bakuya whispered a few ancient tribal words in his native tongue and reached into his pouch. He sprinkled some powdery substance on the top of the con's head, and then spat into his own fist that still clenched some powder. Making a paste, he rubbed it onto the con's neck.

"Man, what you be putting on me?" asked the con, now wondering if Bakuya was just a squirrel in search of a nut, "You don't have no hepatitis do you?"

Bakuya wiped away the paste. The con gestured for his payment and said, "Buckle?"

"Mirror," Bakuya answered. The con redirected his line of sight along Bakuya's pointing finger that directed him to a parked pickup truck's extended side view mirror. There he looked at the where the large congenital hairy nevus had been on his neck.

"Wha'd you do with it?" said the con.

"Gone," answered Bakuya.

"My lady loved that birthmark-tickle-spot during – I'll sue!"

He reached for Muntabbi's buckle but his hand was blocked, "Deal," reminded the witch doctor.

"Oh, maaann, you're no fun. Just no fun at all," complained the con who looked like he was reaching for something in his pocket.

"Get out of here! I saw the whole thing," Gypsy Saladin shouted and came down the stairs from his shop, "Get out from in front of my store. Work another spot." Bakuya braced for impact from the storekeeper but instead, the man shoved the con artist away – a small switchblade that he had reached for tumbled from his pocket to fall through the sewer grate. He ushered the bewildered witch doctor up the stairs and once inside, closed the door behind them.

"I am Saladin. Don't let the likes of him bother you. You have talent I see. Really. Have you ever foretold fortunes?"

Bakuya nodded affirmatively.

ENTRY 13

My safari for the now elusive witch doctor took me through some of the darkest parts of the metropolitan outback. I slowed my car to round a tight forgotten corner and clipped the curb accidentally. The thump of the wheel interrupted a group of gang members and their posse that had been break dancing to rap that blasted from a music player. 'Brawl' versus 'bolt' jockeyed for a decision within their minds. I was a little more at ease when they looked familiar to me and I pulled over, so they could see my driving error wasn't a 'drive-by' in progress. Besides, if they were going to pull any 'heat,' there'd be no chance to drive away clean before they could squeeze off at least a few rounds in my direction.

"Sup here?" asked the apparent leader.

"You seen a guy in feathers around?"

"Hey, it's White Coat," said one of the youths whom I now recognized as one of those Bakuya and I had encountered when we arrived from the jungle.

"We don't hang with that breed," the gang leader said, answering my question.

"Oh, you mean fly bum. Yeah, he was running to Shakedown Street," said another I recognized, "You saw him too," he added to correct his leader's memory.

"I don't help no white coats what's gives shots to me, man," the gang leader announced, then bared the long scar on the left side of his neck for me to note.

"And my first clue to that was my unpaid bill," I politely observed before driving off. Better to leave before something turned ugly over nothing. At least I heard one of his members add, "White Coat didn't out you man, and he only fixed you."

The duplex's living room of the fortune-teller had been turned into a parlor room and Saladin went about setting up the macabre items on the table that Muntabbi was seated behind. He rigged a few trip wires to switches for mildly eerie effects to be used or not, depending on the gullibility factor of the patron involved. Usually the heavy-duty spook shows on Shakedown Street were reserved for those who paid for séances and the like and were conducted in rooms specially rigged throughout.

"You help me find Doctor Nat?" Bakuya inquired.

"Certainly, certainly. But I want you to help me first. Together we can make some dough."

"Bakuya, no bake."

"You're really a witch doctor?" Gypsy Saladin quizzed.

Before Muntabbi could answer, a woman who looked like a floozy walked in with her gorilla. Okay, it was really her husband, who was gargantuan and all muscle - even in the head, except for whatever remnant of pickled brain still worked. This was a given considering the strong odor of old booze that preceded his entrance.

"Ah, a customer," said Saladin, "Welcome, welcome lovely people. How may we help?" His phony smile was wider than the Detroit River.

"My husband and I want to know our fortunes," she said, with a *crack* of her chewing gum on the words "know" and "fortunes." She sat down and crossed her legs, which seemed rather unnatural for this lady – if one would call her that.

"This is so hokey," said her husband.

Before they knew it, Saladin had them seated opposite Bakuya and after giving them fresh brewed tea, dimmed the lights, "My assistant will answer all your needs," he added before departing behind a dark curtain.

The lady held out her hand. The texture and marks etched upon her palm by the years whispered of some harshness in life to those who would just pause to notice, but of which she didn't speak. What could she – or any of us - have been, had life pivoted differently. Maybe if she had just tried one more time, or if the celestial dice tumbled at some needed moment in her favor? Bakuya took her fingers almost reverently, and then holding them gently, closed his eyes.

Saladin mumbled to himself, "Good, good just like I showed you," while spying from behind the curtain.

The floozy was in a playful mood. Half from getting into it, the other half at trying to get her man to get into it, "Will we win the lottery?" she chirped.

"Get the numbers from him, sweety," his baritone voice chortled.

"No gambling wins on tickets," Bakuya said.

"We're going to Vegas in two days, any luck there?" she asked.

"Yes. Much so."

"Ooooh!" she said and shivered.

"But for other sweetie," Bakuya added.

"What?" asked the wife.

"Husband has another lady sweetie he meets," Muntabbi continued, just as Saladin tripped into the room in his haste and said, "He's new. Simple mistake."

"That's --- insane," waved off her husband.

"Card in pocket says, "In Chains,"" Bakuya said, wishing to only tell the truth to avoid any notion that he was causing trouble.

The floozy got up and grabbed at her man's shirt pocket so quick as to rip it right off its stitching and read the business card aloud, "In Chains... Vegas' Wildest Escort Service? *You pig!*"

"No refunds," shouted Saladin who ran into a back room and secured the deadbolts and security chain on the other side. Anger welled from every pore in the hulking husband who, with an animal-like look spoke not, but rather growled one word to his prey slowly and coldly, "Dead."

"Your wife has said so," offered Bakuya in polite reference to the gorilla's impotence problem. It was an honest attempt to smooth out the mess, but only added napalm to the fire, "that is why she hides beneath blankets with your brother."

Her look of fear blended with astonishment, bewildered even Bakuya, as she remorsefully croaked, "He *knows.*" Trying to cover up the adulterous revelation, she composed herself and quickly proclaimed to her husband, "He knows …absolutely nothing about anything!"

"You're fired," called Saladin from behind the safety of the locked backroom door. The witch doctor had no such refuge, as he was grabbed by his arms and lifted from his seat before he could do anything.

LATE ENTRY

I had recognized the officers in the police car as I pulled up. Most cops eventually come into the E.R. at one time or another. They bring in drunks, psychiatric patients or come to take reports of victims of various crimes. Sometimes they are even victims themselves.

"Hi ya, doc," one officer said.

"Either of you guys seen a witch doctor?" I asked, "Feathers, beads, bushman accouterments?"

"I think all those long night shift hours are catching up with the doc, Marty," said the officer to his partner.

"I'll say," Marty responded.

The dispatch radio crackled with the announcement, "One twenty two, civil disturbance involving man dressed like jungle native. One ten Montague."

With the address in my mind, I took off down a side street as the police went their way. Didn't matter though, as we both reached the address at almost the same time. There, they were already out of their vehicles and checked out the front of the darkened tarot card shop. The sign in the door's window read, "Closed."

"Nobody here," I half said and half asked.

"Typical," noted Marty, "Whatever happened was settled and everyone scattered." His partner went up and knocked on the door. While they looked out front, I went around the back into the alley and stepped over a hobo who was as busy mumbling to himself as he was rummaging through the trash boxes on the ground – the poor devil. I saw his friend in the dumpster moving beneath, shifting debris. I slid open the bin's side door to make it easier for him to get out than have to crawl over the top of its rim. It was so crammed full of junk that the trash spilled out along with a bloodied and beaten witch doctor. His limp torso hung half in and half out of the side of the dumpster, trying to look up weakly to see through bruised and swollen eyelids.

"Bakuya," I uttered with amazement.

"Nat. It is good to see you, if I could see, that is," he replied.

"What happened?"

"I was only trying to help some people, I only told them the truth."

I took his arm over my shoulders and pulled him out the rest of the way from the fetid filth. I felt sorry for him. Dare I say, empathy?

"The 'truth'?" I echoed sarcastically, and then having taken inventory of the consequences added, "Welcome to my world."

Often times, it's better to tell people what they *need* to hear, rather than what they want to hear. But that might negatively affect the patient satisfaction scores. That *is* what it's all about now. Forget that we operate in a profession, an environment that is unlike any other business, just... *Have a **magical** day*.

By the time Bakuya and I got back to my apartment, it was early morning. I couldn't believe the CT scan showed he had no facial bone fractures. I fidgeted with turning the key in the lock with my left hand while my right supported a still woozy witchy. The ice pack that he held over his eyes brought the lid edema down just enough for him to see somewhat. As the door opened, he called my namesake insect name as if he had just spied a lion waiting to spring.

For there was no apartment, or at least what I had known as an apartment. It was in total ruins - furniture cushions slashed open, books torn apart, cupboards and shelves emptied of all their contents. The top of the toilet tank was cracked in two in the hallway.

"Evil spirits," Bakuya said.

"You got the 'evil' part right, witchy." At the time of discovery, this was a simple burglary, but upon closer examination of the details, whoever did this had taken quite a long time to trash every nook and cranny – not like a thief who wants fast in and fast out. This wasn't just robbery. Either someone was out to hurt me, or they were hunting for something. Why? And how to find out?

ENTRY 14

The Detroit Greens and Polo Club is like an oasis. Verdant wide spaces for golf and plenty of room for the polo horses, just a diminutive distance from cracked concrete, crack heads and broken hearts. Friendly competitions here are the sidecar for the engine that drives the region's economic deals that are made and business alliances formed. The round that Kels and Mark played was one such example, I learned, when Jeff called me for an update while they were on the golf course together.

"Well?" asked Kels as he selected the proper club for the next shot.

"The witch doctor's okay," Jeff answered, "Nate says we're making progress." (Journal side note: Progress? If I said it, *I didn't really mean it.*)

"Nice day out here, eh?" Jeff continued, "Thanks for inviting me to come out to play with you guys."

Kels pulled a box from under the club bags in the golf cart and presented it to Jeff, "Not sure if you deserve this yet," he said while lifting the lid to show Jeff the polo shirt inside.

"I saw this in the club's pro shop window," Jeff said as he pulled the prize from the box and checked the size. On the left breast pocket was the club's logo intricately stitched.

"They're sold only to members," Mark added.

Before Jeff could fully examine it with the excited anticipation that he was voted *in*, Kels snatched the box back adding, "But, I want the cure and I want it last week. The university is impatient and so am I."

MORNING ENTRY

Oh crud, another *twelve* in the pit to face today. I need to get whatever jungle juice the guys want and get Bakuya out of my bed & breakfast routine. I was so focused on this lunacy that I stopped to retrieve a blanket from the blanket warmer and tossed it to a homeless man, shivering on a cart. I also first should have checked his temperature, as you want to starve a fever. I usually leave such creature comforts to the nurses as we doctors fly around like rabid bats, trying to see the never-ending stream of patients, to find who is the time bomb about to go nipples up. The chilled man may have managed a smile at my kind act, but if he did, I wasn't able to stick around to see. *Ah compassion*, the forgotten art. May its class never be dropped from life's curriculum.

I met Bakuya at the E.R. nurses' station and decided this was it, "Look," I said, "you've pretty much seen what there is, I think it's time for you to come through and hand over the eye of newt, leg of lamb or whatever the cure is supposed to be."

"I haven't learned -," Bakuya uttered, but was cut off in mid-sentence by my abrupt course change to the empty opposite end of the nurses' desk to avoid any excuses. Or perhaps the interruption was Sierra, who caught his attention, "Bakuya?" she called, "I wanted to say goodbye. …I'm going to visit my sister who's undergoing physical therapy and needs another pair of hands at home. Maybe look for new opportunities near her even."

"Pretty Ladybug fly away?"

"For a little. I didn't know if you'd be here when I get back."

I called Sierra over to go help out with a patient exam. It occurred to me that her leaving may perhaps give Muntabbi cause to surrender what the boys wanted. Then again, worse on second thought, it might make him want to stay longer until she returned from her travels.

"At least no one to bark orders at me for awhile," she added to Bakuya, clearly implicating me and my more brash moments. Then I saw that contemplative look on Bakuya's face. *That* look that meant potential trouble.

"Muntabbi fix Nat for pretty Ladybug?" he said as he put his hand into his animal skin bag, but she stayed his hand. She turned after she gave him an impish glance and as she passed me on her way to the patient's cubicle, rapped her knuckles gently against my chest over my heart and said, "You can't fix a part that's not there to fix." If they had further communication with their eyes, it was scrambled and unimportant.

"Nice girl," I said sarcastically, "Nice girl."

"Nat would like Ladybug?" he hurried over to inquire.

"Don't get your rattles in an uproar," I said, "Besides, she still believes in Santa Claus."

Bakuya asked about Santa. I mentioned his connection to Christmas. He then told me about the Christian missionaries - the ones he had previously referred to as a menu item, remember? - and how they taught that "we …all have our tree to bear." I corrected him saying, "You mean, 'We all have our *cross* to bear'." Then he oddly mimicked Sierra's slight and rapped his knuckles against my chest while listening against it and said, "Yes, except you have a whole forest."

Later this particular day I got a strange call from Meg. She asked, "Did the witch doctor call us?"

She could tell by my perplexed quiet that he hadn't to my knowledge and added, "Jeff got a call when he was out playing golf. When I asked who it was they just said, 'Medicine Man.' I told Jeff about it later but he just stared off and asked if anything else was said."

"And?" I prompted for more.

"Nothing except, *'game afoot,'* Jeff told me that it must be that witch doctor trying to call us. The one that pesky drug company is in competition with for trying to get the Goliath cure, he said."

"He did?"

"When I told him I thought *you* had gotten the info, he just, well, he just sat me on the kitchen table, right there on the morning paper and kissed me before I could say anything else."

I thought that this information was interesting but confusing.

"Did you read the Detroit News this morning, Nate? Headline said *Goliath Clears Customs? – Boston airline passengers await test results.*"

The jungle was getting darker.

ENTRY 15

Today was the big day. On the steps leading to the courthouse, Bakuya stopped to study his foreign clothes. He looked rather dapper in his dark suit coat and tie, while he rolled and unrolled the latter and then asked, "Why do men wear cloth around neck that points to their –"

"—Never mind." I said. One always must be careful around the courthouse. You could be passing a judge or potential juror and any misperception could spell doom.

He insisted on coming though I didn't want him. Still, I would worry if he was left alone since nobody would witchy-sit. I had no energy to waste on bothering with Bakuya – this court building is the last place any physician wants to be.

I reminded Bakuya that this time would be better spent studying for re-certing the boards - which we must do every ten years now – than having had to review my previously given sworn deposition. He was rather surprised that although we prove ourselves over and over when already doctors, we are marked 'expired' like a gallon of two percent milk, on an appointed day after ten years. He admonished me to stop lying when he learned that we have to pay a good sum to continue to practice – bills for continuing medical education credits to be met, classes attended, journals to review, malpractice insurance premiums, blah, blah, blah.

Inside the courthouse our every step echoed ahead of us down a long hallway. Then a side door within the hallway opened. It was a nondescript door, the kind you pass without ever thinking that it could be the one you're looking for. There came forth first one bailiff armed with a twelve-gauge pump action shotgun, then another who walked behind him. The sound of moving, colliding metal followed them as the prisoners processed in single file behind them. They were shackled at the ankles and tethered together at the waist by chains that were linked to their handcuffs. The steel gray color of the chains nicely coordinated with their depressed demeanor more than their bright orange jumpsuits with, *"Prisoner – Co. Jail"* embossed on the backs of each, could.

They kept to one side of the hallway as the armed rear guard made sure the line was kept straight. As they passed, for a moment, we unintentionally walked in lockstep as if I was a member in their company. The thought of, *so this is my reward for helping people,* crossed my numb brain. No words were spoken, save for a mumble of surprise from Bakuya at what he had just witnessed. It was a mumble of neither English nor his native tongue. An impossible communication, yet perfection in response, groaning in its tenor, it echoed the despair that was mine to shoulder.

A passing woman with her infant paused to take a cautious step back at the sight of us. She cradled the living innocence that she held all the closer as a prisoner spat against the wall nearest him. We all were that infant once. Do we ever think about what we *are*? Perhaps it would mean so much more to remember what we each once were. The prisoners rounded the corner as I reached the large faux oak doors of my appointed courtroom. Their chains clattered and clanked, each one like an incarnation of Dickinson's ghost of Jacob Marley, departing for courtrooms beyond my view.

Inside my appointed courtroom a jury of sufficiently pissed off people were impaneled by morning's end. Both counsels had questioned them and each obviously hated being there – can't blame them – and thus despised *me* as defendant. Those who could bring themselves to look at me during the selection process spoke with their jaw firmly set and lips pursed, as if they wanted to proclaim in unison, "You bastard, thanks to you, I'm stuck here against my will." It would only get worse from here as the proceedings progressed.

Counselor Calalot was slick and polished. One of those men who's marked his territory in many a courtroom case and was now about to piss on me: "…And so… doctor Nathan Briggs most certainly *did* violate the standard of care." Lawyers always use the word *doctor* with a mocking emphasis in the world of litigation.

I wanted to emphasize how close to *liar* that *lawyer* is to *my* ear. But you are to sit there emotionless, as if pretending to be a Sumo who refuses to be moved. I saw Bakuya from the corner of my eye, sitting forward like a jaguar and waiting for my attorney to pounce just like one of those big cats, yet not understanding why my counsel couldn't since I told him he was there to defend me.

"When he intubated the accident patient," Calalot continued, "he may have protected the airway but inadequately stabilized the neck and he caused my client permanent nerve damage to his arms and legs. That is the reason we are all here today."

A photo poster of the patient was unveiled to the jury. It showed him in a motorized wheel chair with the tracheostomy tube still in the front of his neck. The jury was in Calalot's palm. Calalot bowed his head solemnly and said, "He wished he could be here, but he's awaiting discharge from the hospital after having fought off an infection - a bout of urosepsis from a dirty bladder catheter. A catheter that he now must frequently have." Calalot made sure to position himself where the jury could quite clearly see that he was indicting me.

It was tag-team time. As Calalot sat down with a sadness that came across as faux, his partner, Counselor Johnson, shuffled his papers and stood rather stiffly, "We'd like to call plaintiff's first witness…"

All that first hour the jury was fully attentive. By the time lunch was over and we were back in session, they fidgeted restlessly and fought droopy eyelids, as the plaintiff's witness pummeled me, "…Yes, obviously had Doctor Briggs adequately maintained immobilization of the cervical or C-spine, the plaintiff would not have been injured," he said.

I wouldn't expect anything less from a hired gun. Most physicians refer to a doctor who testifies for money as a 'medical whore.' He hires out his opinion, gets his cash, and slants testimony toward the benefit of the payer. You don't get to ask any questions of them, but if the rules allowed just one query, it would be: *Of course YOU never have been in any tight situations, YOU'VE never been wrong, HAVE you Dr. Quackers?*

I'm not a god. If I were, I'd plant my ass on my own private Caribbean island with a large beachside bonfire nightly: *"Throw another lawyer on the fire, Jeeves. We're out? Fine, a politician will do."*

I shuddered back to reality, as Preston, my attorney, was on the attack with the cross examination of their 'expert,' "You believe my client and not the brick wall meeting the plaintiff's motorcycle caused the specific injuries that plaintiff's counsel referred to? Let's not forget he was moving at fifty miles per hour when he jumped that curb."

"If the plaintiff, Mr. Rogers, says he remembers having no neuro deficits before he passed out at the scene, then Doctor Briggs had to have hurt him."

"You believe a head injured patient with a developing cerebral bleed can be one hundred percent accurate?" Presston asked.

"From the records and the outcome, I believe Briggs was reckless," spewed the whore.

The judge noted the time and rapped the gavel for a recess until the next day.

LATE ENTRY 1:45 AM

I remained sunk in the beanbag-like chair in front of the dark little TV that was 'off.' As I stared at the empty screen, my mind conjured its own show trying to remember how I ever came to do this now accursed career. But the Nassau Royale liquor had already released the coherent thoughts from my grasp and now worked the bottle free from my hand. It fell, empty, to the floor, rolled over some potato chip crumbs and came to rest next to one of Bakuya's ceremonial masks that I had filled with dip. The noise caused Bakuya to come from his bedroom and crank up the light switch dimmer – breaking the bottle over my head would've been less painful than the brightened lights on my tired, unadjusted eyes. Seeming offended, he removed the empty container from touching his mask.

"More in the cabinet above the sink," I garbled, "Help yourself."

"You should be sleeping," he said.

"It doesn't matter, witchy. Nothing we do really ever does, does it?"

He just stood there perplexed. Perhaps at me, perhaps at wondering how to get the French onion dip smell outta the mask.

"Everything we do is for naught, eventually," I sighed, "Great spirit comes and takes us all."

"Nat is scared."

I tried to get up but could only manage to roll over with my butt still in the bean chair as I tried to extricate my stuporous self, "Damn, damn right I am. Everyday. I'm that kid who's scared of stitches. As scared as that person who may be breathing their last." I grabbed Muntabbi's necklace that hung down as he bent closer to inspect me and derided him, "You act like a deity with only worthless trinkets. *Look at me*, I'm a fancy pants witch doctor."

I somehow managed to rise and danced around the room like the awkward, seemingly brainless scarecrow from the Wizard of Oz. Alcohol rants never end well. I've known this from every Saturday night in the E.R. I lost my balance and fell face first into the dip. The 'mask of anger' plastered to my face.

"You wear the Batooksi tribal mask of anger well," he casually observed.

I pulled off the mask, and wiped away the dip from my eyes and nose as I continued my rant of the pitfalls of healing in my jungle that are unknown in his, "Lawsuits, personal, financial, emotional ruin. Friends known, who've suffered notoriety, depression. Suicide! All potential consequences just trying to *help* someone can bring. And if you do make a mistake…" the crumbs of the just crushed potato chip fell from my hands, "…you have to live with it the rest of your life."

"Oh, good. For a moment I thought you'd lament the wrestling-the-drunk-patients, all over again," he said. The jungle man didn't get it or maybe he did and he chose to ignore it. My head banged down against the nearby wall from the weight of it all. I didn't appreciate his little comment and before I could say a syllable or give him a small knock, Bakuya held the mask of anger before the front of his own face for protection. Anger – it didn't fit, it just wasn't him.

CAVE OF JUDGEMENT

New day, but oh, if only it could all be nothing more than just a nightmare. I felt sick to my stomach but choked down some breakfast – on the second attempt, having barfed up the first attempt. Don't want to chance passing out before the jury from low blood sugar, it looks bad. I peeked in Bakuya's room. Crap, I envied him. He can help a tribesman or even just play with his rattles over him, and he will never be made to feel like a criminal assailant. I left quietly without disturbing him, as I didn't need his disruption. Not today.

In the courtroom, Calalot and his partner, Johnson, organized their papers. Calalot looked like he had been up most of the night planning his attack. The two bombastic barristers spoke loud enough, intentionally, just for me:

"I'm exhausted," said Calalot.

"Large award will buy quite a nice rest," Johnson said, looking to make certain I was listening.

Presston arrived and took his seat or rather *reclined* at the defense table. Shoulda been a lawyer. He popped a tic-tac and pulled out the stack of legal pulp that was my reputation, my work, and a part of my life, all reduced to eight and a half, by eleven inch sheets of paper. Then he asked, "Left your friend at home?"

"Yeah," I muttered.

"Just as well. You're going on the stand today."

I pictured how the black flowing robe of the judge could be better accessorized with a scythe rather than the gavel he rapped. The jury filed in and was seated.

The judge said, "Let the record reflect court is now in session and Plaintiff's Counsel may proceed with the next witness." Except he only got the first three letters of the last word out as he sat in awe. Jaws did an upside down stadium *Wave,* dropping around the room before closing again. One by one, first the stenographer, then each member of the jury then...

"Nate," said Presston, to direct my attention to the doors. My jaw dropped lowest. For there in the courtroom entrance between the great oak double doors, was Bakuya, in the most elaborately formal witch doctor's outfit I ever could have imagined. He proudly strode in. His long cape was made of what looked like leopard skin – sure, *that'll* work with any animal rights members who may be on the jury – his chest was covered by a mat of tiny hollowed bone shafts tightly woven together and dyed in individual day-glow colors. On his head was a headdress with colorful striped feathers that protruded chaotically from their golden headband – its surface covered in a nail-punch design of what appeared to be tribal icons. On each of his upper arms was a bracelet from which hung a fringe-like collection of dried black mamba pit viper tails. His face was painted garishly from the juices of whatever fruits and vegetables I apparently had left in the fridge – and some I didn't even know I had. My breakfast thankfully had already left the building – most recently, most colorfully, in the men's room - or I would've hurled right then.

In his right hand he held a staff he had fashioned from a dead tree limb with an equally ornate rattle fastened upon its top. Somehow, someway, he was both garish nightmare and respectably regal. His stride to his front row seat in the gallery, directly behind me, was worthy of a head of state.

"Look!" called out Calalot, "Not only is Doctor Briggs an incompetent, he's partners with a witch doctor."

Giggles and snickers erupted from both the jury and the courtroom spectators. Their mirth at the attorney's mocking insinuation amplified Calalot's half jovial, half forced laugh.

None of this phased Muntabbi, he sat tall and proud, eyes forward. I could only bury my forlorn face in my hands with the dread that I was indeed sunk. The judge tapped his gavel to get the attention of the court over the giggles and guffaws, "I'll ask this room to come to order and I'll instruct the jury to disregard Counselor Calalot's statement and strike it from the record."

I turned and whispered, "Have you been sniffing your own pouch?" But Bakuya remained mute.

"I'd like to call *Doctor* Nathan Briggs to the stand," called Calalot. Did I write that lawyers love to use your title as a slur against you?

Eyes shifted upon me as I moved to take the stand and Bakuya quickly raised a short, straw-like hollow reed to his lips and blew. The tiny poison dart found its mark, in Calalot's ass. He stumbled toward me, his eyelids heavy, "...After a nap," he added and fell. I caught him before he could hit the floor but not out of any altruism on my part. For Bakuya's sake, I took the opportunity to discreetly remove the evidence from the bombastic barrister's butt.

Counselor Johnson was rather bemused, "He did say he was very exhausted."

"We'll take a short recess," announced the judge.

The bailiffs assisted and took the sleeping (I hoped that he was just sleeping) lawyer for some air, attracting the eyes of the court that followed them out the door. I took the moment to ditch the tiny dart into the wastebasket at our table unnoticed.

"Bakuya, do you know the penalty for killing a lawyer?" I asked softly.

"Besides indigestion?" he replied.

"I mean -"

"- Not dead," continued Bakuya quietly, "He will sleep like a baby for hours."

His helpfulness didn't change things. The judge had a docket to keep and moved forward. The plaintiff had arrived and was gently wheeled into the courtroom and looked weak. He didn't look too bad though for just having gotten out of the hospital. His trach tube was long gone and the surgical opening in his neck had appeared to have healed over some time ago. I hoped the jury might take note and realize that the poster they were shown was an old one, one that apparently was taken soon after the accident.

Shortly after the recess at 9:30am, I was on the witness stand. By 2:45pm, I was out of energy and a year had just been washed from my life with the sweat that emptied from every pore.

"So," said Johnson, "You still lifted up on the laryngoscope blade." He wasn't asking, he was *telling* the jury.

"With an assistant holding the head still to immobilize," I added.

"But could this not still allow the neck to move some?"

"Not in this case."

"But in some?"

Ah, he was going to try to open doubt in the mind of the jurors. Get the schmuck on the stand to agree that an action *could* do something and you've indirectly paired *it* and *you* in their minds.

"I don't know about others, I only know about what I did in this particular case," I stated.

"We know what you did in this particular case. My client especially knows." Johnson went and stood next to the plaintiff sitting in the wheelchair off to the side, and added for the jury, "Every time he gets too tired to hobble along with his crutches and must use his wheelchair, *he* knows." He paused for effect and stared at me. "No further questions your honor. Oh, just one more. Did you talk about the case with your friend over there?"

My heart skipped a beat, the letters "OMG" wildly flashed repeatedly in my mind. Because...

"Perhaps you didn't hear –"

"– Yes," I blurted.

"Thank you, doctor," Johnson said. He was elated. Presston glared at me.

When you're sued, you can talk to your attorney about anything. You can talk to your spouse, if you have one. That's all protected. If you talk about the case to anyone else, then that person could potentially be deposed as a witness.

"Any further witnesses, counsel?" the judge asked.

"We'd like to call -," Johnson bent over and whispered to Presston who whispered back, Johnson straightened and announced, "Bakuya Muntabbi."

Bakuya rose proudly and was directed to the witness stand.

"He can't do that, can he?" I begged, hoping that his lack of understanding of our culture, language nuances and apparently, just how much my ass was on the line, would exclude him. Presston just shushed me and waved me off. I made a tactical error, I was trying to be nice, educate the jungle man by telling him probably more than was wise, *never* believing that he would be stepping onto the stand. My mind raced for some answer – anything to keep him from opening his mouth. Since I'm not currently under oath, I thought that maybe I could lie and say from my seat that he was my odd "partner" and thus like any spouse, couldn't be made to testify – no, even *I* couldn't sell *that* one. "We're sunk, Presston. Let's settle. Now. Please?" I softly pled, while Johnson bent over the wheelchair to whisper, "Here comes our slam dunk."

"Do you, Mr. Muntabbi," questioned the judge, "swear to tell the truth so help you –"

"- Bakuya will not lie for Nat."

The seriousness in Muntabbi's eyes caused the judge to instruct, "Proceed counselor."

Johnson now swaggered before the jury. He took his time like a shark positioning itself for the best disemboweling bite. "Mr. Muntabbi, what do you do?" he asked.

"Bakuya does not understand," answered the witch doctor.

"Do. Your job."

"Bakuya no have job, Bakuya is Grand Tribal Healer of the Wammami clan."

"That's your job. Now –"

"- No. That *is* Bakuya."

"Does Doctor Briggs believe in your medicine?"

For the first time, Bakuya painted me with coldness in his orbs. He knew the answer and I was in fear of what he just might say next.

"No." Bakuya answered firmly.

"Do you believe in Doctor Briggs's medicine?"

"Nat has medicine."

"Did you say Gnat?"

Silence. And thankfully, Johnson didn't press Bakuya for an answer likely thinking it was a dialect issue and was happy enough to use it to further downsize me in the eyes of the jury.

"But is it good?" asked Johnson getting back to the medicine question.

"Objection," Presston called, "Vague and ambiguous."

Johnson continued his attack, rephrasing, "Did he tell you if he thought he did wrong? Hurt my client?"

"His mind knows he did right. His heart has become confused and uncertain."

Johnson's swagger was even grander now, "Oh,? And why is that? Did he believe he might have done something wrong?"

"He is a man," said Bakuya, "A good man. Who fears not that the right thing was not done, but rather that it is perceived that he may have been human –"

"– For we all know, to err is human," Johnson mocked.

"But he is not," continued Bakuya, to Johnson's surprise, "Not allowed to be human. He must be… perfect."

I rose slowly. Why? I don't know. My adrenaline was at an all time high. I wanted to run. Wanted to throttle Bakuya, then Johnson. No, Johnson, then Bakuya. Maybe jump out the window to an untimely death – crap, we're on the first floor! But Presston's firm hand quietly held me and guided me back into my seat.

Johnson quizzed, "And did he say he was perfectly right one hundred percent in this case without a doubt?"

Bakuya's posture stiffened at the trap that was set. We both knew the answer. Probably so did the jury by his continued silence.

The judge ordered, "The witness will answer the ques –"

The judge was silenced by the admonishment of the witch doctor's rattle-staff, which he shook admonishingly in the judge's face for silence without breaking a locked focus on Johnson. Bakuya rapped the bottom of his staff with an air of ruling proclamation on the floor twice for attention and then said, "I do not know whether his medicine was correct or not, but that it was… good."

"Good," echoed Johnson mockingly, "We are not here because of *good*. My client –"

"- Is here because of anger," said Bakuya.

"Yes!" Johnson exulted.

"Anger demanding justice."

"Yes!" Johnson repeated and pranced like a cheerleader.

"Anger demanding justice from the intent to do great good."

"Yes! – No," Johnson fumbled, "But obviously, you do not understand. Do you?"

"Bakuya understands –"

"- No further questions for the witch doctor," Johnson interrupted and turned his back on the stand.

"Objection," Presston and I both called out in unison, surprising ourselves that we both spoke and stood at the same time. I quickly sat down to defer to Presston who clarified, "Counsel asked Mr. Muntabbi a question, and Mr. Muntabbi didn't get to finish his answer."

"Counsel must let witness finish his answer," the judge said, "You may proceed Mr. Muntabbi."

Bakuya seethed at the games of Johnson, took a breath and continued, "Bakuya understand *reconcile*. Reconciling one's spirit of caring despite those who would seek revenge. Giving flames of anger back to its fire. Giving the anger of suspicion back to the chasm of doubt *we all* harbor within."

Johnson sneered, "You think me gullible?"

"This is not gullible, nor weakness. To intend good, to do despite risk, is raw courage – strength. His medicine is good."

While the jury was deliberating, we waited. I mulled Bakuya's words over in my head as I imagined each of the chairs of the jury to be wired with electrodes. Not for its individual member, but rather, awaiting me. For whatever one may think of the guy being sued, you can bet he feels like all eyes see him as no different than some kind of monster, a criminal. I'm not certain how comfortable I am with a pole dancer, bartender and assorted other non-medical personnel deciding my fate - although I actually envy them. Whatever vexes them in their day, they can always comfort themselves with the fact that, 'Hey, it's not like it's life-or-death.' Medicine is frequently such. Can they know what it's like to have to make the decisions that I make under the conditions that they're made? I don't expect anyone to understand. You might get a cold reception if you go up to a combat vet in a bar and tell him, "I never served but I know it was rough." Unless you've been in combat, no, you *don't* know. Now, I could only wait some more and hope.

The judge came in and sat down at his bench, silently indicating that a verdict had been reached. Would I be exonerated? Would I be wiped out?

We stood as is customary each time the jury enters or exits the room and sat after they did. The judge asked, "Ladies and gentlemen of the jury, have you reached a verdict?"

"Your Honor, we did."

"What is your decision?

"We find the defendant with… no breech of standard of care."

I almost collapsed. I almost vomited. I almost cried, cripe, I *did* cry. I was seen in the eyes of the jurors as a healer. Not a hurter. Presston patted my arm, but it was to Bakuya whom I turned and knew not what to say. Yet he made no eye contact. He sat, remaining proud and emotionless, ignoring the repeated stares of others. As I turned back toward the bench, from the corner of my eye, I saw him wink without looking directly at me.

"This case is adjourned," declared the judge.

Bakuya got up and walked toward the plaintiff. I gently called his name to stop him, fearing something would still go wrong. Some rewind button could be punched or the verdict in some way amended. But he ignored me, all the while being carefully watched by the plaintiff attorney.

"Bakuya apologizes for your court loss," he said.

Then he bowed slowly and respectfully to the plaintiff. A Madagascar Hissing Cockroach, about six inches long spilled from a fold in his robe onto the table, before the plaintiff. The plaintiff who just a moment before couldn't muster much strength, leapt up and out of the wheelchair to flail his arms and legs wildly like an Olympic athlete as it scurried up his arm. And then he screamed, "What the hell?"

Everyone saw it. Bakuya smiled politely and rose from his humble bow and came over to me.

"He played it," I uttered in disbelief, "How did you know he played it?"

"Bakuya sensed at start."

"Why didn't you expose him sooner? Why put me through that, to the end?"

"Nat needed to win on merit. Not a four foot."

"Forfeit," I corrected, "No one's ever done something like that for me."

"Just did."

"Heck, let's …."

ENTRY 16

"...Celebrate," I repeated over the sidewalk crowd noise outside the Hockeytown Bar - great nightspot and a perfect contrast for a city of contrasts - a bar that salutes the hockey team, right across the street from the baseball stadium where the Tigers play some great ball. I just know they'll put a hockey arena near here one day.

I threw my arm around Bakuya's neck and a couple sporting his and her mohawks gave us a wide clearance. They seemed uncertain about this guy in a suit and tie, who hugged the guy in feathers and bones in a loincloth.

I shouted, "I'm gonna buy you the best meal and then drink until we can find a bison we can take down togeth-"

Life is rude when it doesn't let you finish a sentence. Masked men sprang from a van, parked behind an empty Chevy there on Woodward Avenue. They grabbed the witch doctor and knocked me to the ground, in one swift maneuver. I don't know if they were quicker, or this other car was, a car that appeared out of nowhere and slid in ahead of the empty Chevy.

My brain was addled from my skull having been bounced off the pavement, "Hey! What are you doing? Someone, police!" I called. I tried to grab Bakuya back but received a kick to my aching head for my efforts by one masked man, as another pulled out a Glock pistol from his waistband and squeezed off several rounds at me. I rolled between the empty Chevy's front bumper and the appearing car's rear bumper for shelter. I would've sworn I wet myself. Gunplay ain't like in the movies – *action...adventure...* - no, only fear that you probably won't see tomorrow. I don't know how people like gang members live with that reality day after day. Me? I'd choose another line of work.

I saw clothed ankles and calves from my shelter beneath the parked cars, they quivered and struggled as they fought against those of the resisting witch doctor. Up went Bakuya's feet as they managed to stuff him into the back seat of the appearing car. I sat up as its engine started. The masked driver threw the car in reverse causing me to dearly hug the pavement near the gutter, a tight enough hug to make you think I should've offered it a diamond ring – I think this now means we have to register at Neiman Marcus. The rear bumper slammed into the empty Chevy behind it. I was showered with front-end rust dust and headlight glass from above me and then the car with Bakuya was gone.

The sound of their tires pierced the night like the shriek of a whistling bottle rocket and every bit as fast.

All that remained on the sidewalk besides some blood from my scalp wound was a few feathers, some beads and a broken bone and claw necklace that I gathered up. A bar waiter came up and asked if I was "okay," once he was sure the scene was secure. I could only rub my head and fumbled to pull out my cell phone. I dialed the police and said, "I need to report a… snitched witch doctor." I didn't know why it happened. I kept wondering what else he did while I wasn't with him to make him a target.

I walked into the ER, the scalp laceration no longer oozed blood, though the dried blood down my cheek surprised Nurse Kiley enough to ask me what had happened.

"Somebody grabbed Bakuya. I've gotta find Jeff."

The ER is a funny, terrible place. Some things surprise you. Some things that people shouldn't have to see some times, you see it over and over. Always the same, and yet never the exact same disaster, for it's always with a twist. As if to say, *you thought you're prepared, you bastard? Did you see **this** coming?*

Such was the case as an ambulance crew quickly hauled a stretcher past me through the automatic doors with just another faceless person rendered anonymous by the oxygen mask.

"Sierra?"

Thelma came around her station desk and triaged the patient on the stretcher to, "Room seven. Universal isolation precautions, people." The pain in my head was extinguished by the adrenalin rush and forgotten, I rushed to don protective mask and gloves and plastic gown as the latecomer not understanding why the "isolation" unless it was some kind of Haz-Mat or hazardous materials accident. Everyone else had previously gotten the word and was already in total body condoms. I went in and looked closer. Sierra indeed.

"What's the story?" I asked Dr. Selfridge, who had just finished a quick exam.

"She called one of the nurses to say she was sick and wouldn't be in," he answered, "and then evidently collapsed while still on the phone."

Nurse Candy added, "She just got back from her sister's –"

"– Boston," I muttered, while Dr. Selfridge scribbled orders on the electronic tablet. "I've seen the news reports too," he added, "Don't jump to a conclusion."

If any one's familiar with Murphy's Law – it goes something like, '…the worst thing will go wrong at the worst moment' – you would surmise like some of my colleagues, that Murphy was indeed an E.R. doc.

I grabbed an ophthalmoscope and looked into her groggy eyes then looked underneath her eyelids, "She's got petechiae under her eyelids," I said. Those are little red or purple spots that are tiny areas of bleeding beneath the skin – sometimes an ominous sign.

I let my guard down. Shouldn't have. I shouldn't have let Sierra hear what I just discovered, for I had no sooner noted the finding than a weak voice called from the cart, "Nate." It wasn't a call to me so much as it was a question in search of an answer.

"We won't know until the virology titer comes back," I said in my most professional voice, "When did this start, Sierra?"

"If it's what we think," she half whispered, "will it matter?" Even with this, she still managed a smile. That same smile that she flashed to put me at ease in the heat of battles past. I didn't want that smile, not there, not then.

"Besides, you got me where you wanted," she added.

"Where?"

"On my back."

She closed her eyes and smiled all the more at her cleverness.

ENTRY 17

For the first time it felt a little strange in my own apartment. I flipped off the bottle cap of my beer with the cap affixed on the unopened bottle I handed to Jeff. He didn't need an opener either. That's what his gold wedding ring was for. When, in a relationship, does that symbol become useful as a beverage utensil? Moreover, does it still mean anything when it's reduced to such?

I pondered crap like this trying to flood my mind with other thoughts - anything rather than think about Bakuya or about the virology tests.

Jeff let out a long loud belch after a swallow of brew, "The police haven't found anything yet."

"Finding a kidnapped victim is a little different than finding someone who's run several blocks away, Jeff." My logic was sound. There wasn't anything that I could do for the police in their investigation. There's nothing magical that I can do for Bakuya and the specialist physicians would already be doing all that modern medicine could for Sierra. I watched this logic sink-in, completely frustrating Jeff. He was pissed. He slammed his beer down and threw his head back squirting a thin stream of beer through his teeth straight up into the air like a whale spout, then caught it back in his mouth. He used this talent in college to taunt the home football team when their receiver missed catching the ball. He would enlist the aid of some guileless co-ed, having her chase the stream with her mouth before it fell back between his lips to tauntingly demonstrate to the players that the girl was a better wide receiver. He hoped to piss them off enough to inspire them to get a little tough, he would say. He was really just looking for the nearly always inevitable warm lip lock with the co-ed there on the cold bleacher bench.

He got up and stomped to my door until I muttered, "Someone knows he's got the cure."

"You believe? What changed your mind?"

I didn't answer. Some of the things about the witch doctor I still haven't figured out. Other things played with the one or two neurons that still fired in my brain, "That Doctor Truffle guy. I learned Kels brought him on board personally."

"Turffle," Jeff corrected.

"He used to work for Prism Pharmaceuticals."

"We know all about him. You're thinking too hard, let the police do that, bro." He took another whimsical swig of ale and said, "I hope that E.R. nurse doesn't have Goliath. The way I caught her looking at you at the Kels'. Kind of like she likes you - if you weren't the ass you are."

Jeff left me to my thoughts and his empty bottle for me to collect, or rather, challenge me to collect when I tripped over the coffee table while trying to retrieve it. I fell to the carpet and quickly lifted my hand. Impaled in my palm was that missing claw that I must've dropped from the broken necklace I had gathered at the crime scene and brought home. I pulled it out hoping that its semi-hollow center didn't contain some kind of poison or bad mojo. If it did, I hoped that my end would be painless and quick.

I took the small claw into the spare bedroom and placed it on the dresser with the rest of the broken necklace. A photo that was worn and cracked, with its color fading, stuck out from behind one of Bakuya's rattles that lay on the dresser. I took it for a closer look and accidentally sent the rattle to the floor, where it rolled back and forth. Its sound was like a thousand cicadas buzz-humming as one.

The photo was of some expedition team that had been to their village. Two of its members posed with Bakuya and his family. His children – much younger then – clung lovingly to their father. The shot was by no means a close-up, but there was something there that I couldn't understand, something, some essence within those people that wasn't ever elemental within my life. Yet this manner, this ethereal component, was universal in truth and to them, it mattered.

"It *matters* – to them."

I tied what remained of the necklace around my neck. The ceremonial arm bracelet with the beads that were ripped loose during the kidnapping struggle was now fixed around my biceps as I moved quickly around my room. The pulse in my temple area throbbed as if to the sound of some unseen jungle drum. The rattle still rolled back and forth on the floor to find equilibrium and defied it at the same time.

I made the phone call: "Jeff, tell Kels to let the team know I found the cure in Muntabbi's effects and I'm going out to find him."

SUPPLEMENTAL ENTRY

I drove all along the route of the car that fled with Bakuya, could've taken. The city isn't laid out in a grid like Chicago or New York, it's more like Paris or Berlin where the streets radiate outward like spokes. I pulled up alongside youths hoping not to get shot or carjacked. I flagged down patrol cars and handed out copies of Bakuya's photo.

I even went down where all the hookers hang out. Suggestively clad ladies for whom love never was or shouldn't have been, but now was nothing more than only a business transaction. They've been all over the city but none had seen the native in the photo. Even Eve. So named not because of being a 'lady of the evening,' but because she's the oldest hooker on the strip. I've taken care of her on numerous occasions in the E.R. Once when a john busted her face when he was suppose to "bust out a Benjamin," or a hundred dollar bill, and other times when the protection had failed and she had the venereal disease of the month needing treatment.

I had even resorted to stapling a copy of the photo to a phone pole with a number to the E.R. on it. Nailing my thumb in the process, to her amusement, Eve took another drag on her cigarette, as the street didn't look too promising for customers at the moment. She could read that I was tired and giving up at whatever it was that I was doing.

"Don't give up," she said, and crouched suggestively low in front of me before laughing at either the tease or perhaps to see if a business deal could be done. I *do* have standards, and that includes no hookers or former patients. She threw the remains of her cigarette into the gutter where the rest of her real dignity had sadly ended up long ago, then she felt the cold hard cement with her fingertips while still crouching there knees apart in that almost tripod position. "You need to feel her pulse," she said referring to the concrete and rebar that's the city's backbone, "She knows. You only need to feel her and she'll tell you."

This creeped me out enough to wonder how many hits in life her psyche had taken. I had, many times, seen the crusty, cursing bitch she was. But here was the tender mother that never would be, the wife that never was, relating to the only semblance of 'family' she had that was surprisingly still dear to her, if somewhat broken. Eve wandered wounded in the city like the rest, yet gave me the poke to drive another staple. Ironic, that.

I talked to the fakers and frauds. Careful to avoid the gang bangers who didn't look, at least somewhat, familiar. It's a predator/prey mentality. Some people wouldn't thing twice about taking your life from you along with whatever else they had wanted to claim. To draw a bead on another human is exciting in the movies because few directors have had to face a gun. When you've squished around in as much blood as has soaked through my running shoes, you'll understand that it's life's *elixir* reduced to being underfoot, not some makeup artist's special effects after the gunplay.

"Doctor Briggs," came the voice from behind me.

I turned to see him, the wrist injured patient who tried to scam me for narcs, "*You*," I groused.

"Can I interest you in *my* flyer?" he said holding out the paper leaflet.

"If you're looking for –"

"– I don't need to anymore. That friend of yours... After that buzz wore off, I was cured of my addiction," he said before happily trotting away to press his fliers to other palms. He added over his shoulder, "I'm free. Bless that brother, doc."

Again the witch doctor. Any more of this and I'll be out of business. Gee, what a truly wonderful thought!

SUPPLE ENTRY

Yeah, it's supposed to be 'supplement' instead of 'supple,' but I'm in a hurry and even though it's fruitless, I tacked up fliers near the hospital. The old lady who was on the cart when I had my breakdown was again leaving the hospital. "Hello, doctor," she cackled with the gentleness of your grandmother.

"If you've seen this man anywhere," I instructed, "please call –"

"– Will you dance again?" she asked, referring to my trippin' "Chippendale" faux imitation.

"Have you seen him?"

"I'll see anything if you dance again," she said with a big mucus stringed, toothless smile. I was grossed out, but yet, there was a twinkle in her eye. Not one you can ever see in an old crone, but one that comes from a vivacious young thing. Bakuya told me that eyes outwardly don't change because they're the body's skylights to witness the soul and the spirit never ages. Something I hadn't truly noticed before.

I went around to the back of the hospital and found several winos groggily gathered near a cozy dumpster. I grabbed a large discarded hunk of sheet metal and with a similarly discarded broken mallet handle, clanged on it loudly to stir them, calling, " Rise and whine!"

"Did someone say 'wine'?" asked one of the hobos from a large cardboard box, looking for his next down.

The flyers, crumpled tightly in my now frustrated grip, were the antithesis of these lost lumps of flesh before me that barely stirred.

"Jeff's right," I said to the wino who had no clue about what I was speaking, "this is nuts." I threw the rest of the flyers toward the bums, reasoning that they could probably use a few sheets of fresh toilet paper at some point. As I headed away from them, I heard one of the homeless men behind me stir and say, "Get up. Get up," to the others. "Tha's the doctor what's worked for me in the emergency room," he slurred on.

"Some rich fat cat," came the call from a box resting on its side, followed by spittle hawked out by its occupant from beneath the box flap.

"He gave me a blanket," continued the homeless man, "Clean blanket, like when I was an upright man with a real home. Dignity," I heard his voice trail off reminiscently.

I looked back and saw Rusty, a hobo with a corroded makeshift prosthetic hook hand, fish through crates near the dumpster (he lost his original one as payment for liquor and other substances that were 'procured' for him). "Treated my frostbite last winter," cackled Rusty, "Stitched a wound. Never did pay him." He laughed so hard he gagged then he coughed and wheezed. They watched me as I walked to where I had parked my car and got in.

The occurrence of the next events then happened without a moment to react. I reached to close my driver's side door. A utility truck from who-knows-where bashed the driver's door off the frame without even stopping. Had my hand been grasping the armrest, my arm would've been torn away with the door. The maniac driver never slowed. I looked to get the license plate but couldn't see one. A mini-van with its sliding side door already open, skidded next to me and stopped inches from my now non-existent driver side door. Where did *he* come from? At last, a Good Samaritan. I turned and there in the van's open doorway was Dengon's grinning face.

"Hello. Goodbye," he said, and grabbed me by the shirt and yanked me into the van as it peeled away. The last thing I saw, before the door slid shut, was a derelict walking with a bag lady who pushed her personal shopping cart, just take it all in and ignore it all the same.

ENTRY 18

I was dazed from the punches to the head that I took in the van. Not sure if I completely passed out for more than a second but at some point I decided that to continue to struggle would lead them to make certain I struggled no more. We stopped moving and the door to the van opened. From my vantage point on its floor, I saw we were at what looked like a service entrance surrounded by verdant landscaping and evergreens.

An armed security guard in uniform pulled me onto my feet and Dengon pushed me into the building. We passed through a kitchen where dirty cookware from the previous meal's preparation rested in stacks near a large sink.

"The view outside was nicer," I said.

"Compared to this, or a makeshift grave?" Dengon's dry lips muttered.

I then considered the momentary thug-induced dream I just had recovered from: Bakuya stood in the fog on a street corner outside of a pool hall where gang bangers often came to pre-romance their bimbos.

"You boys," said the homeless man.

The gang leader laughed at the hapless soul's attempt to hail them and called back, "It's 'Yo boyz,' bum," while the rest of the gang chortled smugly.

Undeterred, the homeless man said, "We have a proposition. Rusty will even throw in his best bottle."

Rusty smiled toothlessly while he held aloft a bottle of vino. I guessed that bottle represented the elixir for Goliath - if I was interpreting the dream right. Or perhaps just that I got my noggin knocked too hard.

The gang leader pushed the winos back like bowling pins, "He ain't posse. We don't stick our neck out for nobody like dat." He then made a missile of the bottle where it burst upon impact with the wall. "Don't lick it up all in one place," he snickered to the winos and fist-bumped with the others.

Defiantly, the homeless man stammered back, "You get a wound on your right, to match that scar on your left, who's gonna help you *housey*, who's... gonna... **help**?"

I thought he might help Bakuya in the next mental image but the dream's story clip didn't veer.

"Get off our street," warned the gang leader, as his toady added, "And it's '*homey*'." The gang leader became perturbed at the remark and stared. "*What*," asked the gang toady in reply to the obvious irritation that belonged to his boss.

I was snapped back to the here and now when I was sat down hard on a wooden chair. My head banged so hard against the window behind it that I turned to see if I had cracked it. What I saw beyond the pane of glass in the distance were stalls and polo horses, then a large beast changed the view – more Sasquatch than man – when he spun me around to face Dengon. His facial features belied those of the helpful, friendly guide who was no more. He was angry and didn't offer pretense as he declared, "Bakuya betrayed his culture – my father's ancestors, by sharing his power with outsiders," he said.

"You're one of Bakuya's tribe?" I quizzed.

"My father was banished by his family before I was born. You have the witch doctor's medicine," he continued.

"I do?"

"Which you'll give up unless you'd like to be buried with it."

"Which you wouldn't know about unless you talked to Kels."

"Kels," Dengon deadpanned in a way I could tell he didn't connect what I was getting at.

I believe there's a power sometimes, when you're faced with a situation of which you aren't in control, where you just allow yourself to go with it. You *need* to go with it. So helm that boat over the falls, drag your demons back to hell. What I'm saying is execute some faith, and you'll likely execute your fears. Maybe you'll even get lucky.

You see, I figured the only way to get to Bakuya was by having something *someone* wanted, but few knew of. So I called administration and told them I had the medicine. Who else would've known?

If Dengon was at all curious of my plan, he didn't show it, as he again demanded, "The medicine, Doctor Briggs."

"Go fish," I said.

"What?"

"You have the *bait*," I continued, "*Me*. I was the bait. Only I never had it. I only wanted to find Bakuya."

Dengon took a mouthful from his tumbler glass and spit it into my face. It was a Bloody Passion cocktail - if I was correct, and heavy on the cognac. A backhand chaser to my face followed this. Really, I prefer my cognac straight, without my own hemoglobin, which oozed from my now bleeding mouth.

"Take him to the medicine man," Dengon snarled.

Gee, one day a helpful college student, next day a prick. They blow up so fast now, don't they? You'd probably not ponder that question for long if you then saw Dengon yank my head backward and diabolically trace a line with his fingernail across my throat as if to imply my eventual fate. ...And the crap-nut had a hangnail! It hurt!

ENTRY 19

I was thrust through a pair of ornately carved, oak paneled double doors onto my face. The impact was only slightly cushioned by the expansive Oriental rug before the old massive fireplace, flanked by Tudor latticed windows. I lay there in the private smoking parlor of the Detroit Greens and Polo Club wondering if I could use the chair leg that my head had just finished using as a brake, as either a means of support or a weapon. The chair itself however, was already occupied, "Nat!" came the always-cheerful voice.

"Get him up," ordered Dengon to the willing security guards, "I don't want to have to pay for that bloodied Oriental rug."

Tethered in the chair with heavy tape, Bakuya smiled down on me with his notched teeth still intact from his captive ordeal and said, "I refused to give any knowledge of the potion."

Dazed and tired, I was hoisted and dropped into a chair next to Bakuya and like him, lashed to it with duct tape across the torso, forearms to the arm rests by looping the tape around them and over my lap and continuing across Bakuya's armrests and lap, "I'm having such a bad day, witchy." The guards taped my left leg to the chair leg and in doing so, secured it as well to Bakuya's leg and chair next to me. My arms lashed tightly to the armrests with tape they ran across the space between the armrests.

Over the security guard's handheld radio came the call: "Unit two, please check-in with the sentry at the gate." As they left, Dengon followed them out but not before he picked up a lethally sharp halberd from a suit of armor that decorated the old Tudor manor styled room. He examined the spear-like point at the end of the long thin handle and threatened, "Don't relax, you'll have plenty time to rest, soon."

ENTRY 20

I always knew that Jeff was in my corner and had my back. When I next spoke to Meg, she eventually mentioned that around the time I was confirming to myself there in that old English style room that bondage would never be a 'turn on' for me, Jeff was rushing out of the house and grabbed his cell phone from the lamp table. She had put their cell phones under the mail and "past due" bills, which she had hoped, would remind them to address the paper pile that always clamored for attention.

"Why the hurry?" she asked Jeff.

"Nate's unavailable. Called him on the landline - won't answer. I'll be back," and he was out and away. She wasn't sure he heard her call out, "I'll text Kels' wife: we won't be meeting for dinner." She dug out that remaining phone and activating it, noticed the screen, "Honey!" she called after him, "You got my cell – 's okay, I'll just use yours."

As her fingers began to type upon the screen, an incoming text message chirped and popped onto the screen. She recognized the message's icon as the same crest from Kels' Country Club. Meg tapped the message into view and began to scroll down the lines of elegant font, her face becoming crimson, her chest heaved with each stunted breath. "Oh, no," she shouted to the empty house, before she dashed out the door after Jeff.

Jeff's car was already several driveways down the street when she chased after it, "Jeff! Wait! Jeff!"

If he had looked into his rearview mirror at that moment, he'd have seen her throw his phone at the car where it became an instant kit in a million pieces by landing short upon the concrete. She ran back into the house quickly, but not half as quick as the tears that rolled off of her flushed cheeks.

Back in the private smoking parlor of the Detroit Greens and Polo Club, I glumly looked around the room.

Bakuya broke the silence, "I wouldn't give Dengon the medicine for Goliath. I wonder from whom within this country club it is that the guards await instruction?"

"Kels." I answered and asked, "Why'd your family banish his father, Dengon's I mean?"

"He ransomed our clan's location for a great sum to game poachers – those that would attack and kill us. They would then be free to operate. No witnesses to the poachers' harvesting of slaughtered animal trophies.

He was found out and failed. I'm sorry they got you, Nat.

"I got me." These words puzzled Bakuya and I explained, "I used myself as bait with a bogus story. I didn't think you'd give them the medicine. So I broadcasted that *I* had it."

"Why?"

"- The best character witness a friend could want. --- To find you."

"Bakuya is quite a *character*, it true."

"Here, help me scoot to that suit of armor," I said.

"How?"

"Hop."

Bakuya followed my lead as we bounced and scooted together in our bonded chairs towards the suit of armor. We must've looked pretty stupid the way we scootched along. We didn't care about appearance. With my free right leg, I kicked the suit of armor, it's outstretched arm holding the halberd swayed from my jolt.

"No," Bakuya stammered, "no Ko-koes!" I then noticed that the arm swayed lower and was now perfectly lined up with Bakuya's crotch. Though I tried to kick again, Bakuya bounced with more strength than me – out of fear no doubt. Off my aim, my next ill-placed kick now had the weaponized arm align with *my* manhood and looking to release at any moment.

"Move, move, move," I yelled, scooting all the more. I thought that getting the sharp weapon was our only hope before those screws came back.

"Dangerous," muttered Bakuya of my attempts.

"So's the alternative."

Another kick and the suit shifted from its support, the arm swung wildly... Whose *ko-koes* will it be?

Bakuya landed an off center kick of his own and down came the halberd's ax blade. *Shwoosh-chop!* Embarrassingly as it was, we both screamed like girls as the blade made its mark. The silence was for but a moment, though like a fine wine's bouquet, savored for the few seconds of peace it offered. Then I waited for the pain to hit. It never came. I opened my eyes and saw Bakuya only open one of his, "Two?" he asked looking down at his crotch where the blade had landed just to the left of his inner lap. It put a tear in his loincloth and partially pulled the material revealingly aside.

"*Three?*" I accurately observed and questioned with no small bit of astonishment.

"Good," said a relieved witchy, "Five?" he asked looking things over further.

"Five," I said raising my freed hand and wiggled my almost purple fingers. What tape the fallen halberd hadn't cleaved through, I quickly worked to remove to free myself. It was at that point that we heard returning footsteps in the hall getting closer.

From the other side of the door, we heard one of the guards, "Can't believe Old Eddy had trouble with that decrepit laid off employee."

"The bum," came the reply from his partner.

I didn't know whether to help Bakuya unbind the rest of the way or look for a weapon. Deciding upon 'weapon,' I tried to lift the halberd but its blade was embedded solidly into the chair edge. Free it with any sound and the element of surprise would be lost.

Bakuya insisted, "You must run now."

There was a *click* from the lock. Like the secondhand on the Grim Reaper's timepiece, its cylinder announced "time" to force my decision. It was then that I spied Bakuya's pouch on the mantel and grabbed it.

"Nate, no!" said Bakuya, "They must not mix."

Before the words left his mouth completely, I had thrown the entire contents at the thugs just at they came through the door. The thick powders coated their faces and contaminated their eyes and caused them to cough and sputter. It was I, not they, who was most surprised, "You called me – Nate," I said.

"I'm - I'm a flying gnome. You are free. Free like me to soar," said the guard, "Now I shall fly." He executed the most graceful pirouette – right out the freaking window. Baryshnikov would've approved. The loud crash that echoed below affirmed wings obviously weren't a part of the hallucinogenic package.

But his partner just stood in the room and stared. Not the stare one sees with a hallucinogen, rather actually *seeing* something beyond our senses. A manic-like grin broke across his face, "I can see tomorrow, yeah, that's what I was scheduled to do. Wait, it's next week, now next month. I can... see... the future! Another New Year." His eyes were clearly fixed on something only he was able to witness. "Beautiful," he giggled, "That's who they elected president? Wait now it's someone else. Never thought *they'd* ever win the World Series. Gotta bet on them. Whoa, party." His whole demeanor changed like someone with a conscience or a soul. However, whatever magic there was, it soon was clear that the vision mutated into something nightmarish. "No," he said to seemingly thin air, "I – I didn't mean to do it – I did, but I didn't care." Sweat beaded upon his forehead, the muscles at the back of his jaw beneath his ears firmed as he clenched his bite, "No. I don't deserve that." He then coiled up in the fetal position – knees to chest, one fist above his ear, the other jerked near his mouth in a 'thumb suck' position. He became a quaking ball of terror. "—I -- Don't put me in the box. No! Dark. So dark. Wait – Conflagration!" (I knew not where he had gotten that word only that it was beyond his normal speech, nor did I even know if it was even him speaking it anymore.) "The flames!! I see it all!"

I moved over to him cautiously as he shuddered there staring beyond this world. I had to ask. I had to know, "Lotto, numbers. Can I have the next six lottery numbers?"

Bakuya was the disapproving principal to my schoolboy's humor. His shaman's medicine was used improperly and here I was, the wise guy. However, this is why people who abuse drugs always surprise me. They always tell me, *"you don't see doc, I got problems."* Yes, but now you just have an added drug problem, fool! I try to never sugarcoat life's vinegar – reality – they just don't go well together.

The whimpering lump of flesh that was once the guard gave me no trouble while I untied Bakuya. There was no sense of the combat spoils being turned in our favor for the empty pouch lay at the foot of the hearth. Another foot or so into the fireplace and it might as well finish its usefulness in this life as tinder for the next fire to be started within the hearth.

"If the cure was in there," I said with a nod to the pouch, "it's gone now."

Bakuya rubbed his now free wrists and rose from the chair, "Now," he said, "Now, you have proven yourself worthy Nathan." It was not said with triumph, but a tone of relief, "Not by this moment, but from that moment that you set out to save me – to recover your people, you had the worthiness of the magic that was with you, when life mattered to you again."

"I don't follow you," I said, impatient that he wanted to play Jeopardy when more goons could back up the disabled ones at any minute.

"In the tooth of the giant that roars, is the end of Goliath." He moved toward me, an answer that was always there but not discovered – until now. From around my neck he removed the hollow lion's giant fang from the necklace's setting and showed me the powder down inside its hollow core. It sparkled and glistened like dust cleaved of a flawless diamond.

I thought he'd drop it as the doors burst inward as Dengon and his trolls returned. He saw the tooth before Bakuya could get it back in its setting and snatched it away. He admired the prize and pieced it back together, "My grail," Dengon said admiringly then added, "It will not heal *your* lot. The corporation rep has determined your lives are over."

Guns were drawn. You wonder what went though the minds of those victims you see, at their final moments. Defense? Escape? Peace with their Maker? Hope? For me it was a 'blurt.' Something you say and you're not sure why. Something that just doesn't make sense like, 'mama-go-ferret-face-to-the-banana-patch.' Nonsensical, but more interesting than, "Don't feed the cannibal," that I spouted just then. They looked at witchy for a moment not quite understanding but in that moment I lunged at the thug who accompanied Dengon and bit his hand that brandished his 9mm semi-automatic, only to be swatted off like a stunned fly with a solid hit to my temple.

Bakuya came to help me up. What I thought was the girding of his resolve to fight at my side seemed rather just another lesson to be learned as he said, "Nate, there's something that I tell you."

"I suck as a cannibal?" I was still trying to get my bearings from being knocked to the floor.

"I'm not a cannibal, I never was," he continued.

"Huh?"

"At my village, I tried to tell you the English teacher cooked good. Her food was most tasty. You had set your mind another way. A set mind doesn't embrace truth because it is suspicious against that which is different from what it already believes. And so until you could open to the reality, to change your mind, I wasted such efforts not."

"Do 'em," Dengon ordered.

A large muffled *BOOM* from downstairs in the main clubhouse interrupted our planned demise. Dengon and the guards puzzled for just a moment before the voice over the radio drew their attention away from us, "Security team, we have a breech. Old Eddy is…" We never did hear about Old Eddy, just a weird choking sound over the walkie-talkie speaker. There was a burst of static and then a totally different voice, "Yo, yo, listen up. There's a new DJ in da house."

Dengon ran out in a panic with the necklace. From over the shoulders of the guards who now looked out the window, I saw what their eyes could scarcely believe: a large contingent of hobos and homeless people converged on the club down below. They marched with a sense of purpose in their step and pride fixed their shoulders, conviction firmed each one's jaw.

The programed bravado that coursed along the synapses of the guards' frontal cortex was now thoroughly short-circuited by overwhelming anxiety.

Of course, directly coming to face the spear-tipped business end of the halberd's ax, and the antique spear wielded by witchy when they turned around, didn't help them either. They exchanged but a glimpse, before 'flight' won out over 'fight' and they were out the door in escape mode in the hall, with Bakuya and I after them.

At hallway's end, the top of the staircase opened into an ornately fitted balcony. We looked down onto the dining salon where I saw Kels. He was seated upon a linen covered chair at one of the pompously adorned dinner tables that were likewise covered in the finest linen, blending with the blue bloods as one white-haired woman said, "Everyone is simply aghast at the prospect of Goliath. Talk of the travelers at the Boat Club down in Boca Raton, you know."

Kels's posture amped up the stiffness to match that of his bowtie, "A little secret?" he teased, "I have the cure for Goliath practically in our back pocket." He really should've been watching his back, for behind him came the human wave. The lovely French doors ruptured inward off of their fittings as the hoard of street people, bums, and homeless dregs, streamed in – many sampled the pastries from the tiered platters and the goodness that life could offer as they came – all to the astonishment of the bewildered and frightened blue bloods at the tables.

One late, last homeless person came in. I recognized him as the guy on the street, the guy who had been in the E.R.

"I'm back," he called to the diners, "and I brought my pussy with me!" At this, everything stopped dead for but a moment to digest.

"That's *"posse!"* shouted the gang members who were in amongst the hobos streaming in.

"No. See?" the homeless man corrected, and from beneath his coat he produced a filthy alley cat. Its fur was all matted from the infestation of fleas and ticks. The tabby then sensed freedom and scratched and gnawed to gain his release. The feline hissed and its high-pitched screeches gave everyone goose flesh. Upon its release, it jumped into the wig of a stuffy old crone and pulled it off to reveal her nearly baldhead, as it ran amuck. Over the tables it sprinted, past Kels and Mrs. Mitchall, who covered their mouths in disgust with the club's fine linen napkins, embossed with its coat of arms. More security and employees entered into the now riot of food, fists, rich and poor, the beautiful and the repugnant.

Seeing Dengon rush down the staircase, I tried to give chase but I was too stunned by what I witnessed. Something I never could have imagined. Not thought possible. Could I have been wrong? It was vaguely familiar, the face that I saw. Then possibly, yes, another and yet, still another. One of the faces, looked up at me and said, "Hey, I think *you* fixed my little bro when I shot him in the butt with a pellet gun," just before he was again pulled back into the melee.

"Those were some of my patients?" I asked aloud.

"They have come for *you*, Nate," said Bakuya catching up behind me, "you are now, for this moment, *their* case. Their patient." I had never seen them in this way before. It made me damn grateful – if not a little afraid. Those who cared nothing and gave nothing, why, some even gave venom. They were now seeing to *my* need as I once saw to theirs. At first my grin was incredulous. Then, I felt it usher possibilities of a new foreign philosophy that overtook my skepticism.

Dengon however had already made good his escape through the chaos, artfully moving through the *wealth* and the *want* that tangled on the polished floor. Bakuya and I pushed and prodded our way, bobbing and weaving to squeeze out like shavings through cogwheels. The only mark on us was that left by a blue haired, matronly old duchess type – whom I witnessed to have reached out and tweak a piece of Bakuya-butt as he made his way out the door. He told me that he bruised, she blushed, and that if he so chose - according to an ancient custom - he could claim her as his bride on the spot. …And if she was already married? Dispatch her and claim her husband as 'servant.'

Once outside, we saw Dengon run for a parked car. Bakuya dropped his medieval spear, jumping up to grab a heavy branch from one of the great oaks and swung over onto it. He then stood upon it and ran over the more horizontal branches as if they were some natural skywalk. Some of these were too thin to hold a man's weight should he stop but the tribal healer stepped too fast for the thin branches to give way beneath him. Though still amazed at just how he could maneuver through the branches, I picked up Bakuya's discarded spear from the ground to use as my weapon. Dengon looked over his shoulder into the trees as he had almost reached his car. Bakuya pounced down onto the thief, bringing down our intended prey. The necklace became airborne as they collided and flew from his grasp, tumbling over itself in the air.

From my throw, the spear impaled itself into the tire's sidewall on Dengon's car with a firm THWONK. The shaft intercepted the flying necklace's trajectory ending its flight except for the gentle sway from its waning momentum. I watched as Bakuya stepped away from the unconscious Dengon and, seeming rather entertained at the prize suspended on the spear's shaft, retrieved the necklace.

"Not bad for a city boy," I said.

"Fortunate shot," he replied as down at the edge of the club property, police cars began to stream in heralded by their sirens that annoyed and lights that flashed.

I picked up the car keys from near Dengon's limp hand, and reminded Bakuya that we had to get the cure back, and that Sierra was infected. The keys, however, were of no use with the tire now completely flat. My lucky shot was now of no luck at all. There certainly wasn't any time to talk to the police with a complicated explanation.

"We need horse power," said Bakuya walking away. The other nearby cars weren't of any use either – no one's foolish enough to leave their car unlocked in Detroit, nor offer to loan their ride out. I followed him, for whatever transportation he spied would have to work somehow. It was the first time I gave my trust over to him, but then we entered the stable. Bakuya hopped on that big sturdy polo steed like a western cowboy, which led me to wonder if he ever rode some large jungle animal in the bush.

Once upon the horse, he tightened his grip on the brindle reigns to step the beast over to me. Then turning him beside me, he put out his hand to pull me aboard. I don't ride and I wasn't about to grasp at his beckoning hand, "No way. I'm scared of horses, I've seen injuries that..." My sentence remained unfinished. The echoes of my words barely hung in the dusty stable air when the necklace passed them up as it flew from Bakuya's hand toward me. I reflexively reached out and caught it, the only item that could save Sierra. And it was then – as Bakuya had planned it – that he yanked me up by my gullibly outstretched arm onto the horse's back, seating me behind him as we blew out of the stable at a quick gallop.

I watched from my high – too high – vantage point, several approaching employees got scattered like bowling pins by the bolting, explosive equine.

"I don't like this," I said in a vibrato voice provided by the horse's mad gallop.

He only calmly called back to me, "You should try riding gazelle."

I would catch glimpses of the rest of the ride only when I opened my tightly shut eyes just enough to see when this cruise missile ride might end – one way or another. We jumped over the decorative three-foot rock wall into the street and continued like an errant shot through the surrounding city neighborhoods. Next peek, we passed Detroit landmarks and tall buildings. But dangerously, rush hour was building as well.

ENTRY 21

One driver in his convertible with the top down continually yelled into his cell phone – more passive-aggressively for the car that cut him off, than at the person on the other end, "Great, some idiot just jumped in front of me." Then our horse's rear end was his view as we maneuvered in front of his traffic-slowed vehicle, "Now I just got cut off by a horse's ass! – No, a *real* horse's butt. – No I have not been drinking," he shouted into the phone.

There was an opening and I held on for dear life. We turned, we raced, all through the streets and back alleys and empty lots. Strangely, no one bothered us. No one knew what to make of what they were seeing. Not that I saw much with my eyes shut most of the time.

We pulled *up* outside the Emergency Department Ambulatory Entrance – literally. The steed reared upward on its hind legs as Bakuya pulled back firmly on the reigns to get the beast to stop. There was a throng of people panicked by Goliath who waited to get in. They all shouted, *"We want to be tested. We want to be tested."* That is until they turned and saw us - and witnessed Bakuya tying up the horse next to an ambulance, whose bewildered crew almost dropped their stretcher in disbelief.

My hand was half numb from holding the necklace so tight as not to lose it on the hellish ride. Bakuya ran, I kind of waddle-ran from saddle soreness, into the building and up the stairs. People looked at me as if I surely must've dropped a load in my pants.

I flew into Sierra's isolation room not bothering with the cumbersome masks and gloves that Bakuya fussed with as he entered. Immediately, I was struck by how pale Sierra looked. What made Sierra what she was, was dimming. I've seen this opera before and the final note is never sweet. She was weak and almost a stranger with the knowledge of approaching death now standing somewhere near.

As I removed the tooth from its position on the necklace, Bakuya reverently instructed, "A small amount of the grains on the tongue." At his voice she moved for the first time, just a little, and her eyelids just a little more.

I gently parted her gray lips and though I knew I was trying to help, I strangely pictured myself an intruder. The given grains of powder refracted the available light as if tiny rainbows danced on her dry tongue. Before I could look again, they had dissolved. I straightened up and stiffly rubbed my back – muscles tightened now with every movement from the punishment from Dante's Ride. I handed the tooth and the necklace back to Bakuya and said, "Don't ever ask me to get on a horse again."

A soft toned whisper reached our ears, practically too soft to discern, "A jackass riding a horse. Interesting." It was the most beautiful profanity I had ever heard. "I heard what you did for Bakuya," she continued.

When my smartphone rang on the bedside tray stand, I moved to get it but her words effectively silenced it for me when she asked, "You still got that sailboat picture on your phone's wallpaper?"

"How – how did you know?" I questioned, as I had never showed her the puppy-on-the-sailboat picture to my memory, "How did you know?"

"That you take double cream in your coffee? That you always click your pen three times at the start of shift? And that you *always* wear *stupid*, 'lucky' argyle socks on Mondays?"

I couldn't speak.

"You told me – about the picture."

Okay, so my mind is burning out from the stress.

"The rest," she cooed, mustering her remaining strength, "I saw – I know. Trivia your mind never remembers but your heart doesn't forget."

"You never told –"

"- I never cared for Nate. Bakuya had it right: *Gnat*. It was Nat; the guy I knew was there somewhere but wondered if he would ever be."

"Why didn't you tell me this?"

"Love can't chase. Love, real love, like a gem – waits to be found." She took my hand into her trembling weak one. I tried to discern if it trembled from the words or the illness. As she rubbed her finger over my hand she noted, "Rough. You never do wear gloves when you clean the frost off your windshield after night shift."

She sensually traced her finger along each of my fingers and the spaces between. I've been touched by a lot of women and touched them. Never was so much communicated in so simple a touch as that one moment. Mesmerizing!

"You got this scar when that child bit you," she added as she played a gentle finger footsie.

I don't quite remember breathing just then, but somehow the words came out, "No one," I said, trying to inhale, "touched me like that."

She grew even weaker now from the interlude and said, "I'm glad I was the first." With that she closed her eyes to rest. I moved away to give her a little quiet. Walking to the window I pondered how love isn't mere feeling but *decision*, courage really. I looked out at the 'tribe' about their business and noticed the little things, what each was doing, each life in the light. I looked at my open palm that Sierra had just caressed and a distant jungle drum beat in the pulse of my temple.

Worry furrowed Bakuya's brow as he felt her forehead, "Something is wrong," he said, "She should be better now. She should not have fever."

I spun back and checked her with a bedside digital thermometer. "What? Why?" I asked waiting for the device to take a reading.

"I don't know," he said.

The thermometer read, 104.8 degrees. I rang the call light for the nurse who came in and asked, "What's
— "

" – Call her attending, she's getting worse." Not that he could probably do much for Goliath. "C'mon, " I shouted to Bakuya and rushed us out of the room.

"None in my village have ever had fever from Goliath," Bakuya said entirely perplexed.

I took him to the hospital lab and took some of the few remaining grains from the tooth. I begged the lab assistant to use the spectro-chromatograph to analyze it. She said without a computer order entered she couldn't do it. New policy rules you know. I had remembered our previous tryst and whispered a very graphic reminder of that time into her ear - including that naughty dark secret of hers that would cause her or any sane person to file a change of address immediately. She rolled her eyes but her breathing became somewhat unconsciously heavier and after hesitating another moment, put the specimen on the instrument. Within a few moments the data and its graph printed out.

"The proteins aren't heat stable when dissolved in the body," I noted.

Then Bakuya understood, "It cured everyone in my village *before* the disease progressed to such a high fever."

I logged into one of the computer terminals and checked Sierra's electric chart with it, "She's been given meds for fever control. They're not working."

Bakuya was out the door for who knows what. I went after him. I prayed that he didn't see Sierra's ghost.

The witch doctor darted to the main lobby area. He looked at one of the tall decorative plants and examined its leaf. Next he did the same to another. He bit the leaf of the second plant and rolled it around in his mouth only to spit it out, then with his bare hands, furiously dug into the dirt in the pot. This aroused the notice of a hospital security guard to whom I smiled and awkwardly said, "Psych therapy. Thinks he's a dog."

While the guard worked this over in his mind, Bakuya came out with a wavy root section and smelled it. He squeezed a milky substance from its root and said, "This maybe make it stronger."

"Maybe?" I asked, not happy with the uncertainty. I hoped the lab would provide us a solid quick assurance and back we went.

Upon our return to it, the lab was sealed off. Locked. I read the sign on the door that said the temporary closure was, "...due to spill of hazardous reagent chemical."

"What spill?" I disbelievingly asked a stupefied Bakuya, thinking perhaps he witnessed something there that I had been oblivious to. Even more surprising, the rest of that section of the floor was cleared of all people already, though only the lab was involved.

One of the phlebotomists came around the corner from the floor with the specimens she had collected from the patient units, "Dr. Briggs?"

"Go."

"She's in ICU with barely a blood pressure."

Word travels fast in a hospital. Gossip, in fact, is faster here than texting in some cases. We both knew we were talking about Sierra. Except Jeff, who came around the other side just then, "I've been looking for you, Nate."

There was, "No time, amigo," I told him. No time for anyone except Sierra.   We went into a medication room. Each patient care floor had one with its corresponding computer terminal. I could tap into the main computer from there and access the lab to get the cure's spectrograph information to then reference it with what similar plant data we could find from Internet journals on Bakuya's root.

The monitor screen provided our answer:

NO FILE FOUND

The information from the test performed on Bakuya's sample had been wiped.

"Somebody wrenched all the data," I said, "Gone." I was desperate. I grabbed the tooth back and put a small amount of the grains in a mixing tube from the med room and added enough water drops to dissolve it. "The root," I said like a surgeon asking for a retractor, with Bakuya already handing it off before I could finish. I held it tight and squeezed.

"How many drops?" I asked.

"I don't know, I've never had to add it to the medicine before," said Bakuya who for the first time, looked like he didn't have an answer for everything.

I squeezed a few thick milky drops to cover the scant amount of liquid in the tube. Though I stirred, mixed well, and drew up in the tip of a syringe by pulling back on its plunger – it still wasn't ready. "No time for the FDA," I said – like the Food and Drug Administration would take any less than forever to approve something like this. At this point, it wouldn't matter. It would either work or Sierra died. The hospital could fire me. I could lose my license. That wouldn't matter now either. It was time to practice medicine, bona-frickin'-fide medicine, like a physician and not some medical bureaucrat with a bastard barrister's beak up his ass.

I saw Bakuya was as uncertain as I was about all this when I said, "It's all on hope."

ENTRY 22

It was at this time that Meg arrived at the information desk downstairs in the main lobby. "Ring my husband's office, please," she asked the info desk volunteer, but didn't wait for the call to complete. Instead, she went upstairs after being told by a Housekeeper, "I saw Mr. Logan up by the lab/research area."

Jeff again interrupted us as we tried to exit the med room while he asked me, "Where are you two -"

"- I have the cure. Sierra –"

"- You can't give it to her. It's untested. Not only could that get you suspended but arrested as well," he informed me, "You've been in enough trouble already -."

"I don't care."

"You never did –"

"– Because, I do care. About Sierra."

"Can't let you do that," Jeff ordered. He *said* this, but when you pull out a Glock semi-automatic pistol, yeah, it's an *order*.

"Are you insane?" I asked, now rhetorically.

He only simpered, "You let me down buddy. Thought *you'd* get it then thought *I'd* get it in your apartment, or by the witch doctor himself."

I started to put it together, "Dengon –"

"– Who do you think hired him and the others?" Jeff said.

Bakuya twitched at the betrayal, "You betray friend Nate," as the barrel was being leveled at him.

"Business," came the woman's voice on approach in the hall as Roxie strutted in. Jeff gave her a wink and continued, "The drug company rushing to get their vaccine on the market now has record stock prices."

"What is this stock?" asked Bakuya, but Jeff ignored him and said, "I was paid, very handsomely to get the drug for them, but they'd be just as happy if it never saw daylight under another company, if I couldn't."

Roxie planted a hot kiss on Jeff. He seemed to delight in our reaction and said, "Oh, did I mention there were bonuses as well?"

"I'll get the car," Roxie purred before she scurried away like the rat she was.

The gun barrel was now leveled at the nasal bridge between the unflinching eyes of Bakuya. I had to do something, say something but all that came out was, "I thought you were a happily married man?"

"You saw what I – we – wanted everyone to see. C'mon Nate, you chased tail."

Meg burst in to the med room. She had come up the same staircase as Roxie who was going down. They had to have passed each other on the stairwell. There, Meg would have noticed the woman's smudged lipstick but couldn't have known it was smeared by her husband's affections. "Jeff, no!" she exclaimed, at the sight of Jeff's weapon. Or, maybe it was more at the garish colored lipstick on Jeff's neck that perfectly matched the coating on Roxie's lips. Women do notice that sort of thing - I've had enough face slaps in the past to know.

"More than your share," Jeff said in continued reference to my past 'girl chasing' exploits while ignoring Meg.

"But none of them ever loved *me*," I said, reminding him of Meg's feeling for him.

His posture stiffened and then relaxed. I jammed him with that one, for I could see the monkeys dancing up there, but the organ grinder was dead. Finally he said, "We're smothered in debt. You think I worked all these years for nothing? Hard to even make my Country Club membership that I *always* wanted," his voice almost cracked.

Meg stood motionless, tears in her eyes, "On your phone. I got the text message from Dengon. You grabbed my phone instead. I won't let you hurt them, Jeff. I bet... I *know* we can still find a way out of this."

Then the monkeys attacked.

"Sierra said, 'never bet on loved ones. Bad luck.'" Jeff fired a round into her stomach that knocked his wife backwards.

He was so calm about the whole affair, it was surreal, "I love you, but I'm not rotting in jail," he said and sighed, "Now, the rest should be much easier."

I saw the situation for what it was. None of us was going to be allowed to go. I decided: time to save my own skin, "Look," I told Jeff, "I don't want to die and you can't dispose of two bodies by yourself, let alone three." Jeff knew that I hated to be in tight situations. My moral compass could slightly spin a few degrees off course if I thought it would save me grief. "I've been trying to get this psycho shaman outta my life anyway," I added.

"True," Jeff observed, "But maybe, I'll just kill you last. Tell me briefly of your potion, Bakuya?"

The witch doctor mumbled to him about herbs and leaves. I saw on a crash cart near the doorway our one possibility and slowly moved about it while Jeff rolled his eyes weary of Bakuya's double talk. Jeff re-aimed at Bakuya's head, "You can just keep it in your grave."

Thump was the soft gentle sound made by the syringe with succinyl choline – the paralytic medication used for rapid sequence intubation – that was plunged at an angle by my fist into Jeff's external jugular vein, its plunger driven downward by my thumb. I swung his arm away for but a moment. Jeff was stronger than me and any attempt to fight him would have been foolishness. The brief struggle only lead to a spilling of the cart's RSI Box - from where I had gotten the syringe - onto the floor. Before I could move any further, he threw me to the ground and put the gun to the back of my head. I made my last thought a good one. As he went to pull the trigger he couldn't. He couldn't move a finger, couldn't stand and couldn't breathe – literally. The paralytic had taken effect and Jeff went totally flaccid.

I punched the "CODE BLUE" button on the wall to summon help and the call with its location was paged over the hospital ceiling speakers. I checked Meg's pulse – it consisted of weak beats and erratic enough to know she wouldn't survive, and I then grabbed an ambu bag with its facemask.

"What is that?" asked Bakuya, staring at Jeff's limp body.

"A paralytic. He can't move a muscle including his diaphragm but is fully conscious to know and hear everything. At least until he dies of asphyxia from not being able to breathe." Then I bent close to Jeff's ear and set it right, "Never bet on a 'friend' I believe is how it went, not 'loved one,' but what would *you* know about that?"

Jeff's flaccid body started to turn dusky blue. I began to breathe for him with the ambu-bag/mask with oxygen from the crash cart as Muntabbi withdrew his hand from another smaller pouch hidden in his clothing.

"Meg's not going to make it," I said, trying to save him the trouble. That's why I figured I might as well work on Jeff. Sucks, but, it was the right triage. Ya know, if Jeff lives, he'll be really pissed when it's time to make a nice "friend" for some big goomba in prison.

Bakuya ignored me and applied a dollop of salve to her wound that seared shut as he mumbled something foreign and put a liquid in her mouth.

The Code Team, along with Security, rushed up the hall with a stretcher to take over the resuscitation efforts. What next occurred there in the hall made me consider using the ambu-bag and oxygen on myself, as I've *never* seen anything like that nor could have conceived it possible. Meg took a breath, then another deeper one.

The witch doctor then softly said to me, "There are still things *your* world is not yet ready for."

ENTRY 23

Leaving Jeff and Meg with the code team, Bakuya and I sprinted for Sierra's ICU bedside. She was already on the ventilator with peripheral intravenous lines in her arms and large bore central lines in her collar bone area for intravenous access. A Foley catheter urine collection bag hung from the foot of the bed that hadn't been emptied and remained bone dry - her renal function shutting down. We had rushed in without any protective isolation gear. I twisted the syringe's tip-lock into the I.V. tubing port and pushed it before any other staff could react. Fast or slow, who knew what was right or safe? More importantly, what would work?

We watched, waited. Her tachycardia on the monitor began to slow a bit, speed up, and then slow again. Then slowed a little more. We prayed it would stop before it dove below fifty. It did, at sixty-two beats per minute. The automatic blood pressure cuff inflated and deflated to flash an increased number from the dismally low number it had been. As I stood for a moment at the foot of the bed, I felt wetness down my sock and into my shoe. The urinary catheter bag's drainage tube wasn't clamped closed when it was last serviced and drained itself of urine that had finally come from Sierra and soaked my foot. I wondered what Sierra might say if she knew she was technically peeing down my right ankle. But I never mentioned it. This time, at this moment, it was welcome liquid sunshine to me. She would hopefully survive now.

I found my breath to finally relax for the first time in days. Heck, first time *ever* in the hospital and walked with a, step – *squish* – step – *squish,* fashion towards the window. The sun seemed exceptionally bright. Down below a police officer pulled Roxie from her luxury vehicle that had been boxed in by police cars. I wonder if she was thinking at that moment what she could've had, being the possible heir to a pharmaceutical fortune. But for many of us, we just never can get enough.

ENTRY 24

By the day, Sierra's color improved and the machines began to come off over the couple of days that Bakuya and I debriefed our souls:

First the ventilator was removed after she was extubated...

"So Bakuya, you came all this way to save people not of your tribe?" I asked him.

Nasogastric and suction tubing – discontinued...

"I came to save Nate's spirit," he replied.

The central lines and I.V. pumps were taken away...

Bakuya added, "Because you have the great healing spirit."

The remaining gear left the room and soon, so did Sierra...

"As a shaman, you, Nathan, are a part of my tribe. And to save one's tribe is to save oneself."

ENTRY 25 (LAST ENTRY)

He had crashed into my world when we had crashed onto his muddy shore. So much I wanted to be rid of him and he knew this, yet he stayed for he said a dry tree loves water yet a storm must first bring the rain. Now that the time had come to take him to the airport, I didn't mind that he had come at all. I once read a quote by Richard Bach – "Every problem has a gift for you in its hands." In this case it was true - I believed it was true and would work to make it true if it wasn't.

I was able to see Bakuya, in his tribal splendor, past security to the gate, by claiming that his English wasn't "perfect." Nobody at Metro Airport could speak his language. Thankfully the TSA agents at the security check points didn't ask me to speak proper tribesman. I admired the awful, disapproving looks from strangers as we made our way to the gate. I now saw my face in those faces. But they weren't given the gift of learning about, or from, the man whom they saw in feathers. Dr. Bakuya Muntabbi truly was strong, smart, and unwavering and you had to be to survive in the bush. He was also a gentleman, honorable, and – God help me - a great physician in his own right. Ironically, he used tools that many would consider weak at best, those weapons of 'genuine compassion' and 'truth,' to conquer the harshest of jungles – ours – that made him the wiliest of savages few could hope to successfully challenge. When we reached his flight's gate, I handed him his boarding pass and said, "Here you go. You should be home by morning."

"Thank you. I hope you visit again," he said.

"I always do what I need, to pay the rent."

He paused and looked as much into himself as he did me, "You hate what you do. But it is not the rent that makes you do it, it's because….it is good. There is hope when people look inside and do what is good. Yes. You are… good."

"Nobody swallows that today," I said, feeling what it must be like for a son to inform his father that he doesn't believe in Santa Claus, yet wanting to.

"You are right, it only works if *you* have the courage to act on it. It is only when we mend others that our own wounds heal."

"Here's a little something extra," I added and pulled the almost forgotten small three-ounce flask with a yellow liquid from a brown bag. Bakuya unscrewed the top and dipped his finger in and put the drippy digit into his mouth tasting it. He beamed, "Wolverine urine!! But you told me there were none in Michigan."

I put my hands matter-of-factly in my pockets, "Detroit Zoo. I pulled some strings. Hope it's enough. More and I wouldn't have gotten it through security."

"It's plenty for our needs."

Bakuya gave me a tribal "man-hug" almost breaking a rib and then departed with his belongings and wolverine pee down the jetway. He waved until the door was closed.

No sooner was the plane in push back from the jetway on the tarmac than my cell phone rang. "'Lo," I said and listened, "What," I told the rep on the other end, "I can't be maxed out on my First Banker Credit Card!" then I remembered something about him later telling me of a man at the front door and giving him what turned out to be my info. In my head, a one-word scream echoed for a week, *Bakuya!*

POST JOURNAL ENTRY

Six long months after saying good-bye to the witch doctor, I planted a warm kiss on Sierra at the top of the stairs as we de-planed with the rest of the passengers. The heat was stifling. Once at the bottom of the plane's steps, we paused near the airport building, where we scanned the colorful faded poster ads for the local fancy resorts. We looked into each others' eyes and smiled.

It was a bumpy ride to our accommodations and we were both glad to finally hop down from the donkey cart. There, in Bakuya's village, was an unexpected warm reception. Exotic flower petals were strewn over our heads as we walked down a short path to a hut. On the door hung a sign with crude letters that spelled, *Honeymoon.*

Sierra's smile sparkled as much as her new wedding diamond in the sunlight that filtered through the tree canopy above like nature's spotlights.

"Just don't pinch any guy's bottom unless it's mine, okay?" I begged her.

She grabbed my hand and we scampered into the hut, then the guard, posted there by Bakuya, closed the door. After all the escapades, this was first love, and though at times we were noisy on the inside, outside somewhere in the distance I heard the witch doctor shake his rattles vigorously, this time, in joyous triumph.

THE END

A Personal Note From TJ Westcott

Thank you for reading Diary of a Witch Doctor. If it gave you a measure of enjoyment, I would greatly appreciate if you'd be kind enough to take a moment and leave a review at Amazon. I am pleased to hear from my readers and you can find me on Facebook or via my Amazon Author's Page.